AF433726

Lives in Time: Part One

Lives in Time, Volume 1

J.D. Ray

Published by Hope Island Publishing, 2023.

LIVES IN TIME: PART ONE

First edition. March 12, 2023.

Copyright © 2023 J.D. Ray.

ISBN: 979-8215941379

Written by J.D. Ray.

For my wife Jennifer, whom I love to the moon and back.

We do things best when we do them together.

And for the contributors at

Writing Forums (www.writingforums.org).

With great patience and stamina, these folks made my writing better.

Cover by MiblArt (miblart.com)

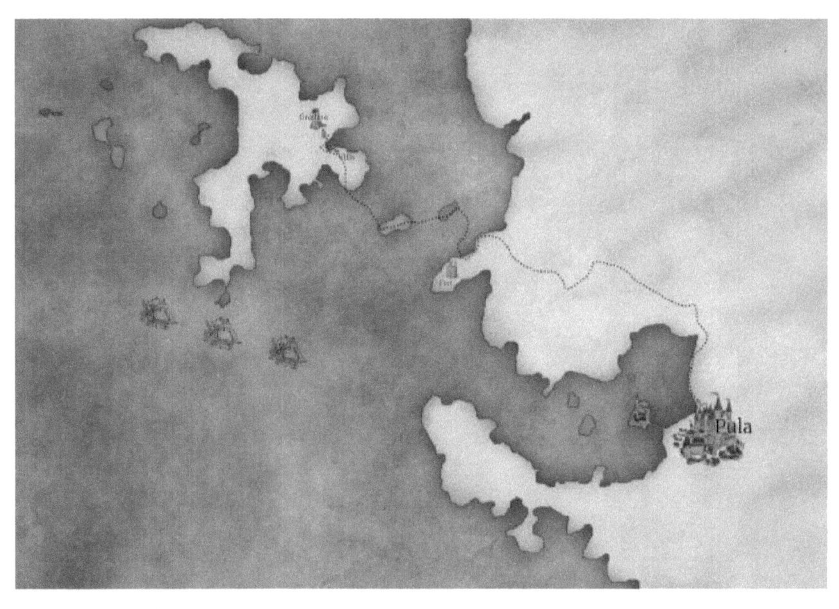
Grahate
Port
Pula

May, 2285

Marko Horvat watched the landscape roll by as the train wound its way through Slovenian farmland outside Koper. He listened idly as his traveling companions chattered away and tried to focus on the farms, the river, and the hills that passed his window as they climbed out of the relatively lush valley into the drier, scrubbier forest that made up most of the Istrian upland.

He did his best to meditate away his excitement, and wished for a view of the sea, which always calmed his mood. So much careful planning went into this trip. Despite himself he felt nervous about finally undertaking it. The sun warmed the skin of his arm, and he rubbed an old scar that tingled in the heat, the result of a long-gone wound.

A pause in the conversation drew Marko's attention.

"So, your nephew is named Marko Horvat, just like him?" A gesture indicated Marko without including him in the conversation. "And he's only sort of your nephew, because it's a large family, and while you are related, it's something like great-grand-nephew, twice-removed or something."

"Something like that," said Marko's wife.

"Zia, don't you find it a little weird that you're introducing me to someone with the same name as your husband when I have the same name as you? Your name is Celestine, my name is Celestine, *his* name is Marko," again with the gesture, "and your sort-of nephew's name is

Marko. It all sounds very confusing." The dramatic tone in the young girl's voice, uncommon for her, showed Marko how nervous she was.

The girl, nineteen, was brash and confident most days, but Marko knew that underlying her bravado was a certain nervousness about the way the world worked. Or, more pointedly, how the way it worked contrasted with the way she thought it should work.

Marko looked between the two women, one in the prime of her life, the other in her golden years. His gaze dwelt for a moment on his wife's face, as it often did. Her well-tanned skin, just starting to wrinkle, told the story of her life. If he closed his eyes, he could map every crease to the time it appeared. He watched her eyes, alive and penetrating, like that of a fencing master giving a lesson to an acolyte.

She had foreseen this conversation, and smiled wanly. "Cele, my dear, names are just names. In my lifetime, I've used many, each when they suited me. If, as I suspect, you like young Marko's company and choose to spend time with him, we'll figure something out. And anyway, we're coming to the end of our lives, and you're just starting yours. Who's to say how much longer such confusion might last?"

At this, she looked at Marko with a smile. To an observer, the smile might have been to share a grim joke, but for him, layers of wry irony, deep knowledge, and a touch of sadness combined to communicate what ten minutes of talking could not. A flush of warmth grew in his chest as he contemplated the depth of his love for this woman. He could never put words to his feelings for her, but they were vast as any sea he had sailed. And he knew his love was reciprocated. Time and grand adventures together secured that knowledge for him.

"Oh, Zia, don't say such things! You're not even three hundred years old yet, still living full lives. Don't borrow trouble!"

Marko smiled at his wife and turned again to the window to watch the landscape scroll by. How much longer would they live? While he was satisfied with what they accomplished in their lives, he didn't feel ready to pack it in. He and Cele had plans for the coming summer, but nothing beyond that.

His mind conjured images of adventures not yet undertaken. He spotted a pair of goats standing on a boulder along the railway, watching the train. One used a meter-long horn to scratch its flank, never taking its eyes off the train. Marko stared at them as the train drew near. One made eye contact and seemed to wink, as if it knew something he didn't. What could it be?

September, 2285

The late summer sun set on the waters of the Adriatic, creating an ocean of fire against a soft background of pink cotton clouds. The boy Marko lay with his head in Celeste's lap, wishing for this moment to last forever. She stroked his hair gently and hummed an atonal lullaby from last year's Bollywood hit soundtrack.

"You know," he said absently, "the name 'Celeste' is kind of common," referring back to a conversation on their first meeting. "If we're going to be together forever, I should come up with a nickname for you."

Her hand barely paused. He detected it and smiled to himself. "Forever is a long time," she said. "We have at least two centuries of life ahead unless The Plague gets us. We've known each other for five short months. I love you, Marko, or think I do. But I'm not even twenty years old and neither are you. Do you know what you're saying?"

He lay silent, watched the sun sink into the sea, and gave thought to what she said. The suggestion she needed a nickname had been intentionally provocative, but now the subject of a life together had been broached, and he found himself teetering on the edge of oblivion.

The summer had been one of perfect romance. His aunt and uncle introduced him to Celeste Foscari earlier that summer. They found one excuse after another to visit the family estate, two hours by rail from their home in Trieste. Each time they came, Celeste came with them. Her parents even came along once. The families promptly decided to refer to the older couple as "the elder Marko and Celeste," as if the younger couple's pairing had been a foregone conclusion. Marko and Celeste "the younger" spent the summer roaming the estate, racing kayaks on the sea, and telling each other stories over pints of beer at the pubs in Rovinj or Peroj.

"Wear sturdy clothes!" admonished Marko the Elder.

"For a picnic?" replied the Younger.

"You're going adventuring, right?"

"Well, sort of, but…"

"Adventures require sturdy clothes. Picnic at the villa, a history tour up at the *gradina*, and an afternoon pint at the pub just north of there before motoring home. Sounds perfect to me."

"*Gradina*?" asked young Marko. "What's there but a bunch of old graves? That's not romantic at all… I mean… well… it's her last week…"

"Young man, have I ever steered you wrong?"

"No, sir, you haven't."

"The *gradina*, then. It's a magical place."

THE old man stood next to his wife on the manicured lawn on a point of land that jutted into the sunlit waters of the Adriatic Sea and waved to the young couple boarding the launch. The elder gave a nod, a gesture that the younger took as acknowledgement of the fun he and the young lady were going to have on their adventure. But the old man knew what was in store for the young couple. He also knew how little prepared the youths were for what was coming. Beside him his wife smiled, but he could see the tears on her cheeks.

She reached for his hand and squeezed it hard, a silent request for him to lend her strength. He squeezed back, let go, and with an arm around her shoulders, pulled her protectively close. If anyone saw and wondered, they didn't ask.

THE six meter launch, a classically-designed boat styled after the yacht tenders of the mid-twentieth century, yet full of modern technology, motored along the coast as the young couple cuddled together on the plush bench. Waves slapped gently against the hull, and the prop made a rude noise with each rise. The motor ran silent as the nav bot worked its way around the many commercial and pleasure craft sharing the popular route. Marko watched as a fisherman pulled up a bass or mackerel large enough to make two good family meals, a rare sight even after decades of careful fisheries management by the UDNG.

"This is lovely," said Celeste, a certain wistfulness in her voice. "How far did you say this boat would go on a charge?"

"Papa and I took it up to Trieste and back once without plugging in or letting it rest, just to see if we could. We took it slow the entire trip, running at about twenty knots, and just barely made it back. It took four hours each way, which didn't leave us much time for having fun in the city, but it was a good trip anyway. I remember lunch being delicious."

"Knots...?" she started. "Never mind. What I really mean is, this trip is well within range?"

"Twenty kilometers or less each way, so yeah. We could even run over to Pula if we wanted."

"What's in Pula? I mean, I know where Pula is, but I haven't been."

Marko thought of the grand Hotel Riviera Pula, restored to its pre-war beauty by some philanthropist organization. He and Uncle Marko stayed there one night on yet another adventure, really just one of his uncle's business trips with a heavy helping of the old man's panache. Marko couldn't remember sleeping on a more comfortable bed. It was an experience he would like to share with Celeste. Forcing his voice to stay steady, he said, "We could go for dinner, maybe some dancing. The boat doesn't care if it's dark when we return." She looked at him quizzically, and a small smile crossed her lips before she looked away.

About twenty minutes into the trip they came to the northern tip of the Brijuni archipelago. Marko instructed the boat to plot a course close enough to the shore to see the beauty of the national park as they worked their way toward the southern end of Brijuni Island, the largest in the chain. In the twentieth century, a dictator had made a holiday home and private zoo of the island. After he was deposed, and his tiny empire broken up into culturally-representative nations, Croatia turned the island into a national park. Two hundred years later, the descendants of the imported zebras wandered the island, drawing visitors from all over Europe and further abroad.

A large offshore breaker rose and knocked them off balance some. Marko held Celeste with one hand to keep her from losing her seat and lunged for the picnic basket with the other. She laughed, and he told himself he could listen to that laugh for centuries.

Ten minutes later, the boat rounded the point and pulled into the small cove named Verige Bay. "Please take the helm," said the boat. Marko moved to the pilot's station and steered toward a good landing spot.

"Grab the end of that line, and when I hit the beach, jump out and hold us to shore while I drop the aft anchor." Celeste grabbed the end of the indicated rope and stood on the bow, ready to leap. As instructed, when the keel hit gravel, she used forward momentum to propel herself through the air where she twisted to land backward, facing Marko. She took a little bow and smiled, hauling on the slack line to hold the boat fast. Marko's heart raced with admiration. He quickly set the aft anchor, then took a hammer from the toolbox, unclipped the shore stake from its holder, and jumped ashore himself, graceless but effective. After driving the stake into the beach, he tied the bow line to it while she waded out, leaned over the gunwale, and retrieved the picnic basket from the belly of the boat.

Sloshing back to shore, she thrust the basket at him and said, "Lead the way, Captain."

Later they basked in the sun against the warmth of a stone wall, a remnant of an ancient Roman villa, and watched a loon dive after lunch of its own in the shallow water of the cove. Marko stared at the label on the dusty bottle of wine he'd retrieved from the cellar at home, bottled in the Croatian Uplands near Zagreb before the war. They'd consumed about half of it with lunch, an aid to digestion and their general sense of wellbeing.

"So what now, Steward?" Celeste asked.

"I thought my title was Captain."

"Times change, we must learn to adapt."

"I suppose you're correct," Marko mused. His uncle's suggestion rang in his ears, and he weighed it with his other options. "The old man practically insisted I take you up to the gradina, which is just a few hundred meters up that hill over there." He punctuated his statement with a gesture toward the trees across the cove. "It's kind of neat," he said tentatively, "a burial ground and temple or something from the Bronze Age. There are trails, and a few signs that give you what's known of the history of the place."

"That sounds great, let's go."

Hiding his surprise, Marko packed the picnic basket and stowed it back in the boat. He checked the shore stake, made sure nothing would get lost if a strong wave came along, and returned to find Celeste putting on her boots. "They dried almost completely," she said. "Socks too."

They hiked around the point of the cove and along the old Roman road on the other side, past the ruin of a small stone jetty, until they came to a place where a trail led into the woods. Marko knew it to be one of the access trails to the gradina site, though a sign clearly pointed the way.

As they walked through the woods, they saw a stark contrast between the Roman stonework of the shoreline and the earlier fortress works of the indigenous people. In some places, limestone blockwork supplemented natural walls; in other places, only one or the other stood to repel insurgents. The trail led up a switchback between two natural pillars, which would have provided controlled access to the summit. The short hill made for an easy climb.

At the top they poked around the ruins and read the plaques to learn what was known about the people that built and inhabited the place. On one sign, a hologram projector showed a short movie depicting what life might have been like there. Celeste marveled at the etched symbols in the stone, snapping pictures with her hand slate. "My cousin does embroidery," she said. "It's a hobby I don't have the patience for, but maybe she can use some of these in her designs."

It didn't take long to cover the entire site, and soon they saw as much as they could. "About half a kilometer that way is Neptun and Istra," Marko offered, gesturing toward the northwest.

"What are they?"

"Hotels. Or one hotel merged from two old ones," Marko said in what he hoped was an offhand tone.

She looked at him curiously. "It's a bit early in the day to get a hotel, isn't it Signor Horvat?"

Trapped! "What? Oh, no, according to my uncle there's a good pub there. I thought we could get out of the heat and have a pint of beer." Ha! Trap avoided!

She looked at him blankly. "Uh-huh." She held his gaze for a moment and said with a wry smile, "Well, if it's beer you're interested in, then I suppose we can get you what you want. Is it beer you're interested in?"

Uh-oh. "I... um... I'm interested in whatever lets me spend more time with you, my dear."

"Well played, Signor Horvat, well played."

With that they began picking their way along what appeared to be a little-used trail in the direction of the hotels. The trail twisted and turned a few times, following the landscape, and eventually petered out. "You seem to have led us into nothing," taunted Celeste.

"I was following you."

"That's barely an excuse," she retorted, her eyes alight. "How far did you say it was to that hotel? That beer sounds better all the time. And after that, we'll see."

"See?"

"We'll see," she said with finality and started back the way they came. "I think this is where we should turn," she said at a large standing stone. "This seems to be some sort of waymarker." He noted that her sense of where they were headed was vague at best, but kept his mouth shut. Further along what could have once been a path they found another, similar stone, this one with carvings on it much like the ones atop the hill. Further yet they encountered two stones, about shoulder width apart, clearly at the end of the disused path. A short cliff ensured they wouldn't go any further without risk of injury.

Marko struggled to decide whether teasing her that they had become further lost would ruin his chances for whatever "we'll see" meant when Celeste said, "What do you think is in there?" She pointed at what appeared to be an opening to a cave. He pulled his slate from his pocket and turned on the light, shining it into the darkness. She did the same.

"Spiders, perhaps a scorpion or two," he said without much conviction.

"You'd better watch your step, then," she said over her shoulder and made her way into the cave. Marko began to protest, then followed. He shined his light around the walls, which were covered in carvings both ancient and modern. Clearly the human desire to leave a mark on the world was deeply ingrained. He saw carvings dated in every century from the eighteenth to the current one. A heart symbol into which someone had carved "M+C" held a place of prominence.

Celeste's hand slate flashed as she took pictures of the most ancient of the carvings. Marko pointed out the heart to her. "Take a picture of this one." She looked where he pointed and laughed. It was undated, but clearly old. She snapped several pictures.

The cave continued deep into the hill. It seemed like a natural cave that had been worked so the walls were smooth. The ancient carvings continued, but the deeper they went, the less they saw modern graffiti. At the end they found a circular room with a high roof and a soft sand floor. Footprints could be seen where travelers wandered into the room, walked around some, and left.

"I wonder what this place was," Celeste said.

"I wonder too. It seems kind of far from the rest of the village to be anything of use to many people. It's certainly someplace special, though." He watched her turn as she took a panoramic shot around the whole room, her slate flashing rapidly as it added light to each segment.

As she completed her turn, she faltered some. "Marko, I feel kind of woozy."

He stepped forward to catch her, and felt dizzy himself. "I feel it too. There might be a gas pocket here; bad air. We should get out." He grabbed for her arm, but let go immediately as he turned to retch onto the sand. She followed suit, and they both fell to their knees, violently discarding their lunch. Darkness engulfed them as the lights on their hand slates went out.

"Just great, I can't see a thing," said Celeste, and punctuated her statement with a spray of spittle.

"I can't either, but I can find the way out. Here, take my hand." Reaching for her, he grasped her hand, struggled to get up himself, and then pulled her up. They were both panting with the effort. "My slate is dead."

"Mine too. I wonder what happened."

"I have no idea, but we should get out. Here, it's this way." He held her hand with his right and found the wall with his left. The way in wound around, but it was a single path with no branches. Getting out would be easy.

After a few minutes they found themselves at the mouth of the cave. "What the heck?" he exclaimed as they made their way into the open. He stood at the cave entrance and tried to understand what he was seeing. "How long were we in there?"

"What do you mean?" asked Celeste. She had dropped his hand in the anteroom portion of the cave when she could see by the light coming in the mouth, and now pushed past him.

"We couldn't have been in there more than an hour. But look, it's morning; the sun is just coming up over the hill."

"Maybe we passed out and didn't realize it."

"That has to be the explanation. What else could it be? It's definitely morning, there's dew on the ground."

They made their way along the path back the way they came. Celeste said, "Marko, something is wrong."

Something else, he thought. As if things weren't wrong enough already. "What is it?"

"I can't say for sure. But these trees don't... they don't look the same. Something is different."

The couple made their way along the path back toward the top of the hill. "We need to return to the estate," said Celeste. "Something strange happened to us both; we'll need to go to town and have a physician check us over."

"We should," said Marko. "There's plenty of charge on the boat to get us back quickly, or we could go over to Pula and see a doctor directly. That would be quicker." Marko's mind raced to try and absorb what facts he could from what he saw around him. The sound of cicadas, usually a quiet background hum, was nearly deafening. The air smelled strange; far more fragrant than he remembered. Had he suffered a stroke? How would he know? He tried to remember his First Aid training, but nothing about strokes came to mind. Maybe that was a symptom.

"That's the better idea," said Celeste. "And on the boat we can charge our slates and call everyone to let them know what's happening. What do you think happened? You mentioned gas, or bad air. Why would that affect our slates?"

"I have no idea, and I don't want to let my imagination run away with me." Thoughts of a nuclear strike rushed into his mind, and he fought them back. "Let's just get to town and figure it out then." Marko desperately wanted to panic, but it would serve no purpose. Forcibly he pushed down the fear rising in his chest.

After a moment, Celeste said, "Marko, I'm sorry if this has ruined your plans."

"Plans?"

"I thought maybe you had... romantic ideas about spending the night away from the estate."

Marko paused a minute before answering. "I admit to having a few ideas to suggest, but nothing that you could call a 'plan'. But no matter that, we need to focus on what's in front of us."

As they crested the hill, they both stopped to stare. Everything, it seemed, was changed. A bush stood where the holographic projector should be; the groomed trails were gone, and the signposts too. The ancient ruins were there, but nothing suggested humans had been in thousands of years save a single bit of weathered ribbon tied on the branch of a tree, and that hadn't been there just hours before.

He stared at their surroundings and Marko noticed that in addition to the cicadas, the sounds of other wildlife were much more prominent; birds sang and bushes rattled, where before the forest was silent save for the wind in the trees.

Thankfully the trail they originally came up from the shore was still there, clearly worn but not improved any, as if the park service was never there. Without a word they ran down the trail, leaping over boulders and dodging around tree branches. They passed between the pillars, which were notably closer together, and bolted toward the road, where they burst from the trees and came to a stop. The asphalt path was replaced by a laid stone road of about the same width—barely two meters.

"This is fucked!" shouted Celeste after a moment to catch her breath.

Marko looked at her, momentarily shocked by her outburst, then across the cove toward the ruins of the villa and their picnic spot. "The boat is gone."

Out of breath, they took off at a trot along the stone path toward the ruins. Those, too, were clearly different. Walls stood at full height where before they were short, the barest remnants of their original construction, and part of the huge mansion was still intact, perhaps even habitable.

The place where they'd eaten lunch was inside a standing building, though the roof tiles were mostly gone. A deer walked from behind the building, saw them, and bounded away. Marko had never seen a deer before, though he'd heard about them being seen up in the mountains where they were re-introduced.

"Fuck!" shouted Celeste. "Fuck, fuck, fuck!"

Marko looked at her, looked around the villa, the cove, and the fields beyond. The scale of what he saw before them threatened to overwhelm him, and he grasped for words to describe it, failing. "Yes," he said quietly, otherwise at a loss. "Fuck."

June, 2283

"What are you doing?" asked Karlo.

"Trying to solve a problem," said Marko. He stood atop a pillar, one of several of various heights in a rough circle. "It's another of the old man's puzzles."

"What's the prize for succeeding?"

"There is none."

"I thought he gave you some sort of reward for being successful at these things."

Marko cocked his head at his father. "When I was a child, Papa, I needed prizes for motivation. I'm seventeen now, and no longer a child. Success is its own reward."

Karlo opened his mouth to respond, then closed it and said nothing. He watched for a moment, then smiled and walked toward the house as emotions wrestled in his mind. No longer a child, indeed.

"I have no idea where we are or how we got here," said Marko.

Celeste looked at him blankly. "I clearly don't know either. This is beyond anything I have the toolkit for understanding." She turned, looking around the area, trying to find something... anything familiar. She saw an olive grove in the distance, but didn't remember it. Was it there before? She didn't know. "Fuck!" she shouted.

Marko looked at her as if she were a stranger. "We may not know where we are, but between the two of us we should be able to solve the problem. We need to focus on what's in front of us."

She considered his words. Though it pleased her to tease him about his age — he was a whole four months younger — she admitted that few others had his strength of character. As they got to know one another over the summer, she found him to be an amiable stoic. Little bothered him, or at least that he showed, but he wasn't stiff as a board like some she'd known. Instead he appeared to go through life with a curiosity about him, welcoming new things without necessarily seeking them out. And he was brilliant. When she watched him play chess and go with his father, with the bold stratagems, the easy dismantling of tactics, he was profound.

She felt safe with him despite their situation, however you might explain it.

"How do I even describe this?" She felt sick to her stomach. "Clearly... well, okay, it seems we're on the island from this morning. Or from yesterday. Or... I don't know. The island, it looks like the same one." She gave him a hard look and waited for his response.

"I agree. And this villa: it looks not-as-old as it did... earlier. It's like everything new is gone; like we've been thrown back in time."

Time travel. Could she believe in it? Was it possible? She thought back to her science professor talking about quantum physics, about how scientists and mathematicians still only knew enough about it to know they didn't know enough, and he was fairly certain nothing would change. And there ended her learning about quantum physics and science in general. At some point you had to realize that there were limits to what you could understand, draw a line, and move on. And subjects like business, economics, and politics were more to her interest than unknowable science. For everyone, she told herself, there were limits. Her stomach growled. "One thing I can say for sure, I'm hungry.

I left my lunch in that cave, and that run down the hill really took it out of me."

As if in response, his stomach growled too. "Yes," he said, "we need to have food." He shrugged a daypack off of his shoulders and opened the top. He took out a bottle, handed it to her, and reached in to pull out a handful of packages. "I have that liter of water, a small bag of almonds, and four snack bars. It's about a meal's worth of food."

"I'm not picky, let's eat," she said. He handed her the almonds and held out the snack bars for her to choose from. She grabbed one at random and peeled back the wrapper. "Not bad," she said around a mouthful. "I wouldn't want to live on them, and they need a little salt, but they're not bad."

"I thought you said you weren't picky."

She looked at him. She couldn't tell if he was teasing, and decided to take the middle path. "I'm not picky, but that doesn't mean you don't get my opinion."

"Fair enough," he said and tossed almonds into his mouth.

They ate the rest of the meager meal in silence, and resolved to save half the water until they found a reliable source to replace it. When they finished, she asked, "So what else is in that pack of yours?"

He gathered the food wrappers and stuffed them in the bag along with the water bottle. "Not much. I have a folding knife, a map of the national park here, which seems now like it might be useless, a light jacket, and a pair of socks."

"Socks?"

He shrugged. "Socks. I'm sorry it's not more."

She thought of the satchel she'd packed. "It's better than what I have," she said with a wide-eyed look. "I brought a few things, but left them on the boat." She watched him shoulder the pack and considered what to do next. She hated being dependent on anyone, but this situation was completely outside anything she encountered before, and she wasn't above asking for help when needed. "So, what now, Scoutmaster?"

He looked at her ruefully and smiled. She liked that smile, and the confidence behind it. She had been fearless her entire life, or so her parents kept saying with chagrin. But she wasn't always confident that she knew what she was doing, content to just do things and let them work out for better or worse. Marko, however, appeared confident in himself most of the time, and she liked that.

He pointed south. "I think we should go over there. You can see Pula from that shore, and that should give us a better idea of what we're up against."

They walked in silence about two hundred fifty meters to the next beach. She'd seen the map of the island, a strange amoebic blob of smooth nodes jutting out into the sea. At a guess, a two-kilometer walk along the shore would get them to where they were going by cutting across the field a few hundred meters. The entire island seemed to be like that.

They reached the far shore and all thoughts of seeing Pula went out of her head as they watched a huge wooden ship sail around the end of the island about two kilometers away. It had two masts, one in the front and one in the middle, with brightly colored sails and baskets at the top of each with people in them, and a smaller mast in the back with a triangular sail on it. It looked like something straight out of a movie where pirates battled the English in the Caribbean Sea.

Someone in the basket on the front mast shouted to someone else in the other basket, and they relayed the message down to the deck. Celeste looked, and could see a person... a sailor, standing at a large steering wheel make adjustments. She guessed they must all be sailors. The ship responded to the command and turned away from the island, crashing through a wave that began to break to the right of the ship. It was a complicated system compared to the automated pilot on Marko's boat.

As they watched, two more ships rounded the end of the island and followed the first. A sailor on the back of the first ship waved a flag as if signaling the ship behind it. Celeste noted what looked like weapons mounted on the front and back of the trailing two vessels, though none seemed to be in use. These three ships were traveling together, the second two likely an escort for the first one.

"Navas," Marko said.

"What?"

"They're called navas, I think. If they only had one mast, they'd be cogs. These have fore- and mizzen-masts, so they'd be navas. Or carracks, I'm not sure. The second two have armaments on the foc'sul and poop decks. Protection for the first, I think."

"Mizzenmast? Fock-sul?"

"The mizzenmast is the aft-most mast, the fore castle is the platform on the front, and pronounced 'fock-sel' in sailing parlance. At least in English. Or so I understand."

Celeste stared at him in amazement. "You certainly know a lot about ancient sailing vessels. Where did you learn all that?"

"Papa taught me to sail. We live on the sea, after all, and he thought it would be good for me to know. And it gave us something to do together. And the old man took me to a sailing history museum in Venice one year and showed me models of all the old ships. I guess it all sunk in." By 'old man', she knew he meant Marko the Elder.

Celeste watched as the ships sailed toward the mainland. Was time travel really possible? Had they been thrown back in time after all? And how was it that Marko had just the resources they needed, and the knowledge when asked? It all seemed too perfect. Maybe she passed out in the cave and was dreaming instead. Maybe she'd wake up in the hospital, Marko by her side having waited there for her, and the world would be back the way it belonged.

Smiling to herself at the girly romance notions, she decided that yes, this must be a dream, and she would just let it play out and have a good tale to tell when she woke up.

But then... how could she know about the anatomy of a ship?

"I can see Pula in the distance, past those two small islands," said Marko, pointing to where the ships disappeared. "We can find help there, I think."

"First, how do we get there?" she demanded, and immediately regretted the confrontational tone. "I mean, we don't have a boat."

"We could swim for it. Those islands are only a few hundred meters away, and the mainland is only a few hundred meters past that. We can rest on the islands."

She peered at the island between them and the mainland. "It looks like a lot more than a few hundred meters to the closest island, but not as much as a kilometer. It's probably less than two in total. I can make it if you can."

"I can make it," he said, again with his confidence. "There's a little island off shore of the estate, little more than a rock—not even any trees on it. It's about a kilometer out, and I swam out there one day, rested some, and swam back. Once we get to that island, we can rest as much as we need before going on."

She thought about getting to the island, and then to the mainland and what they'd do from there. She looked at Marko, and then at herself, and said, "Let's assume for a second that we are, in fact, somehow back in time. I'm not yet convinced that this isn't all some dream, and I'm going to wake up in a hospital somewhere. But for now, let's work through this. So we swim to that island, and then to the shore. Then what?"

"Then what?" Marko asked, looking confused. "Then we find help."

"Help for what? Look at us, and the way we're dressed. If we are not in our own time, what sort of help do we ask for?"

"I..."

"And furthermore," she said, interrupting his answer, "who do we ask for the help? And how do we explain our situation? They would kill us immediately if we said we were from the future. I seem to remember the middle ages as a time when they burned people for saying the wrong thing, if indeed this is the middle ages."

Celeste stared at him, challenging him to come up with answers. In the back of her mind, she worked to come up with a test to determine whether or not this was a dream, but she couldn't devise one.

He stared at her and seemed to consider what she said. "I think we need to come up with a plan," he said finally. "And you're right, we need to be cautious. Unless, of course, this is all a dream and I'm lying in a hospital bed somewhere."

"Well, that would help some," she said.

"Help what?"

"If you were the one in the hospital bed. I hate the idea of being the damsel in distress. It's straight out of some twentieth century testosterone film, when women were seen as needing a man to rescue them."

"Ha!" he said and grinned at her. "If there's any rescuing to be done, I hope it's you rescuing me. I'm feeling kind of at a loss right now."

Celeste proposed going straight back to the cave, but Marko reminded her of how sick they'd been. He said they needed to be better prepared for what came their way, particularly that they needed lights of some sort. She thought, but didn't say, that his curiosity was getting the better of him; that he really wanted to see what was on the mainland. She was a bit curious herself, but didn't say that, either.

They sat on the beach and formulated a plan, working through all of her questions, including some new ones. Marko's concerns were more tactical, and hers more strategic. In the end, they worked out a general scheme of if-this-then-that to use as an operational framework, and agreed to stop occasionally and reassess whether things were working. None of it would be easy, but if things went even reasonably their way, they would survive long enough to gather some resources and come back to the island where they would try to return home.

Relenting, Celeste hoped that on their return they would go into the cave, pass out, and wake up back in their own time. Of course, that presumed time travel was, in fact, in play here, which she hoped wasn't the case. Whether she woke up in a hospital bed or in the cave itself ceased to be a priority for her. The more she could feel the beach gravel on her feet, smell the sea air, and observe the world around her, the less convinced she was that she could imagine all this in such detail.

When the sun began to settle into the sea, they made ready to swim to the first island. A flock of tiny birds flitted back and forth with amazing unison in the evening light, apparently snatching insects out of the air. Marko's backpack was watertight and would act as flotation if one of them needed it.

Celeste watched Marko as he took off his boots and socks and stuffed them in the backpack. She did the same, still watching him as he took off his shirt and cargo shorts and stuffed both of them in with the boots. He stood there in the setting sun wearing only swim briefs, which he had of course worn under his cargo shorts. His level of preparedness was maddening.

She paused momentarily, then proceeded to take off her own shirt and shorts and hand them to him. She saw him look at her and blush slightly. She looked down at herself and tried to imagine what he saw. The matching black pieces, trimmed in lace, contrasted excellently against her olive-toned skin. She thought they looked alluring without being tawdry, which she didn't think he'd like. Did he like it? Was he embarrassed? Did he approve? She stopped herself. She wanted Marko to be attracted to her, but she certainly didn't need his approval. On the approval front, the fitter at the boutique in Trieste would have been horrified that Celeste was about to swim in the sea wearing such finery. She thought about making the swim nude, but wasn't sure that would go over well either. In the end, Marko liked her choice in fancy underwear or he didn't. And if he didn't, well...

She looked up and met his eyes. "What, you think you're the only one who can have ideas?" That, she was certain, would give him something to think about. The idea of spending the night on the island, away from the families, had been a good substitute for her initial idea that they escape into Rovinj. She thought of her satchel in the cockpit of the boat, packed with necessities for an overnight stay. That would have to wait, though, until they figured out what was going on.

She turned away from him and waded into the water. It was cool on her legs, but not uncomfortably so. A few meters out, the sea floor dropped away sharply. She pushed herself off with a kick and began a slow, measured stroke that would get her to her destination with a limited burn of energy. Besides the snack bars she'd eaten, all she'd had since emptying her stomach in the cave was a double-handful of too-green figs they'd picked near the villa ruin. Figs were full of energy, but she expected to be ravenous by the time they finished their long swim.

"*Kojim putem do Pule?*" asked Marko. The man stared back quizzically. "*Da li je ovo put do Pule?*" Marko tried.

"*Stranci?*" asked the man.

Marko looked at Celeste, then back to the man. "*Da.*"

The man looked back and forth between the two travelers, peering at them suspiciously in the darkness with particular focus on Celeste. He pointed down a road and said, "*Onom cestom, a zatim skrenite desno*" before disappearing into the night.

"What was all of that?" Celeste asked.

"I asked him for directions to Pula. He wanted to know if we were foreigners, and I told him we were. That seemed the best explanation. He said to go down this road and turn right. He wasn't more specific; I hope there's a sign."

Both of them had endured the swim well. The water was chilly, as if it were early summer, but not so much that it sapped their strength. From the midway island where they rested, they could see the lights of a defensive fort on the peninsula where they were headed.

As they rested, they talked over what soldiers might mean to them, and how they might change their plans to avoid them. More than a hundred years after the Treaty of Amman, soldiers were something that the lesser nations — or, rather, the nations that were not the UDN — kept in case The Last War turned out not to be, in fact, the last. The UDN had the national police force, and could respond in case there was some sort of internal emergency. But forts on borders, manned (and Celeste pointed out that it was *all* men) by guards wary of invaders was something long gone from the world.

Risking discovery, they swam to the base of the cliff below what appeared to be an outpost, separate from the main fort, then made their way along it to a beach. Marko shook the water from the pack and opened the seal. Everything seemed to have stayed dry. He fished out Celeste's clothing and handed them to her before retrieving his own. Clothes in hand, he stood watching her in the moonlight, which glimmered off the water and made dark dapples against her skin, flickering up and down her body. He reminded himself to breathe as a small knot formed in his abdomen.

She looked at him, smiled slightly, then returned to dressing. He returned her smile, then forced himself to go about dressing as well. Once ready, they followed the road toward what might have been a small village.

The road was deserted and the area eerily quiet, so when they encountered another traveler, all three were startled. Marko covered his surprise and asked for directions, unsure if the man even spoke the same language. After the exchange, Marko wanted to get to the safety of Pula's crowded streets. He couldn't shake the feeling of being watched.

The moon shone down from a clear evening sky and made travel easy. No more than an hour from their encounter with the man on the road, having passed many alleys and lanes along the roadway, they came to a major intersection with two branches to choose from. A signpost clearly displayed directions and distances to several destinations in either direction and back the way they came. Marko couldn't make sense of any of it, and decided to take their guide's advice and turn right.

A horse drawn carriage appeared around a long, sweeping bend in the road ahead of them, and Marko pulled Celeste to the side as they passed. The driver of the carriage stared at them as they passed and said something Marko couldn't make out. He watched the carriage disappear into the night. The driver stared over his shoulder as if seeing something that shouldn't be there.

"We need different clothing," said Celeste. "If we keep what we have, everyone will stare at us like that."

He wanted to provide a solution, but didn't know how. "What can we do? We have no money, at least not in any form we can spend here. And we need to eat. I don't know about you, but I'm famished."

"I am too," she said. "Let's get into town and see what's there. Maybe an opportunity will present itself."

Along the road they passed a few more people in small groups. All gave them a wide berth and long stares, and several genuflected as they went by. The ruin of a Roman amphitheater loomed to one side and the road bent away from the sea. A short distance further it became a boulevard with well-lit buildings on either side rather than the row of imposing walls and iron gates that were previously featured.

"Look," said Marko, pointing across the street. A sign on one of the buildings read *Sobe, Camere, Zimmer.* "They have rooms for rent. Isn't *camere* the word for 'rooms' in Italian? *Sobe* is Croat."

"It is. And I think the other word is German, though I'm not sure."

Marko looked at the building. Three stories tall, large windows were evenly spaced across the front on the first and second floors. On the ground floor, a medium-sized door and two smaller windows with iron-bound shutters. The plaster and stonework were well maintained, and the upper stories were painted a ruddy earth color in contrast to the buildings to the left and right of it, which looked blue or gray in the low light. "It looks reasonably safe. And, as they say, *tko ne vaze, nema blaga*."

"And that means...?"

"'*Nothing ventured, nothing gained.*' Let's go."

Celeste reached for the door handle, then paused. "You should open the door for me," she said.

Marko frowned. "What? Why?"

"If we are, in fact, in a pre-industrial version of Pula, then society is heavily weighted toward the male gender. A duality of patriarchy and service existed wherein women had very little public independence with a man present, but the man was expected to make that situation better by doing things like holding doors and being protective." At least her study of history and sociology was finally useful for something other than academia.

Marko just stared at her as if he didn't understand what she was saying. "That sounds terrible," he said finally.

"I'm certain it was," said Celeste. "At least for the women. The men seem to have had everything they wanted."

Marko leaned past her and reached for the door handle. "I don't know a lot about psychology, but I suspect the men only *thought* they were getting what they want. I can't imagine wanting a subservient life partner."

She thought about the African Republic, the Latin American Union, and Real America with their outdated, patriarchal ideas, not to mention the Arabian League. The UDN, China, even Russia progressed beyond their pre-Enlightenment ways before the Last War. More than a hundred years on, most of the world's population, thanks to South India's membership in the UDN, lived lives of equality.

The door opened into a small lobby about three meters on a side. The walls were decorated with rich fabrics and ornate furniture filled the corners. A young lady, near Celeste's age, sat at a desk. She stood up when the couple entered. Before the young woman could speak, Celeste said, "*Buonasera. Abbiamo bisogno di un pasto e di stanze per la notte.*"

The girl looked at Celeste and Marko. Her eyes widened as she saw their shorts and bare legs. Stammering slightly, she said, "*Bonum vesperam... um... buonasera. An ignoratis...? Sei... straniero?*"

Oh, good, thought Celeste. *She speaks Italian, or something close to it. Latin?* It reminded her of a trip she once took to Sardinia, where the dialect was ancient. Continuing in her native tongue, she said, "*Yes, we are foreigners. We were... set upon by... ruffians on the highway and left with almost nothing.*" She gestured at her own clothing and at Marko's. "*We were happy to escape with our lives.*"

The girl looked at Celeste strangely, but seemed to get the basic idea. She looked down at a paper on the desk, then back up at the travelers and asked, "*Are you married?*"

Celeste's mental gears came to a halt. What did being married have to do with anything? Her own words from moments ago, when she told Marko about the patriarchal medieval society, echoed in her ears. Similarly, there were strict social rules about sleeping arrangements. The girl must want to know if they need one room or two. "*We are not. This is my... footman Marko. Do you have a two-room suite? He can make a bed on the carpet.*"

At this, Marko said, "My Italian isn't great, but it sounded like you just said I would sleep on the rug."

"Hush," said Celeste. "I'll explain it to you later."

On hearing this exchange, the girl looked startled and took a step back. "*Are you English? Do you bring the Plague?*"

Celeste stared at her, wide-eyed. The Plague, a virus devised and released by a faction of radical Chinese ideologues toward the end of The Last War, targeted the long-life genetics of the upper classes. Those genetics, and access to them, was one of the major social issues behind the war. When the wealthy could extend their lives to three or four times the lifespan a middle-class person got naturally, let alone the shortened lives of those who were poverty-stricken, civil unrest was not far behind.

Celeste found her mind suddenly crowded with questions, all trying to get out at once when it struck her that maybe the young woman meant bubonic plague, known in medieval times as The Black Death. "*Wha..? No, no, we are not English! I am... from Trieste... and my footman's Italian... um... Latin is terrible, but he can speak English, and so we use that.*"

At this, Marko said, "*Sì... il mio lingua de Italiano es... non è molto bene... <er> buono.*"

The girl looked at Marko and back to Celeste. She rolled her eyes and giggled, then said with a smile, "*Well, at least he's handsome.*"

Celeste peered at Marko, giving him a dubious look and sniffed slightly. "*I suppose so, given an appropriate light.*" Marko, thankfully, stayed silent.

"*May I have your name for our registry?*" the girl asked Celeste.

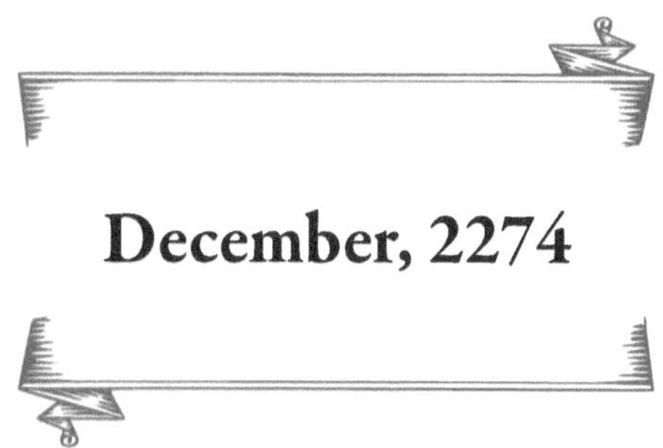

December, 2274

"You must know your family history, Cele. You are a Foscari, and your family was very prominent in this area as many as a thousand years ago."

"Oh, Zia," the girl said to her godmother, "how do you know so much about history? You are old, but I don't think you're a thousand!"

Celeste Horvat smiled at the girl, just nine years old. "Yes, Cele, I am old, and no, I am not yet a thousand years and probably never will be. But I have studied history because it helps me know people. And knowing people is more important than knowing anything else."

With echoes of her godmother's advice fresh in her mind, Celeste squared herself in front of the girl and said with a definitive tone and just a touch of authority, *"My name is Celestine Maria Foscari,"* emphasizing each element with clear enunciation.

The girl stiffened in clear recognition of the name. *"Foscari?"* she asked.

"Foscari. You may have heard of my family."

"Yes, yes, my lady, I certainly have. And my family is pleased... very pleased to have you and..." she looked at Marko, uncertain. *"We are pleased to have you and your employee stay with us. I will speak to the kitchen and find you a table in the dining room if you like,"* gesturing to a door to the left of the entry.

"Thank you, but the... mishap on the highway left us... unfit for public view. Can you have something sent to my suite?" She tilted her head slightly at Marko. *"My footman is capable of serving dinner."*

The girl gave a quick curtsy and disappeared through a door behind the desk. The clang of cook pots could be heard when the door opened. After a moment, Celeste could hear a male voice. She couldn't make out his words, but he was clearly upset and seemed to be telling the girl *"no"*. Then Celeste could hear the girl say, "Foscari", to which the man replied, "Foscari?" and continued to say something in what must've been a more calm manner, because Celeste could no longer hear the exchange.

The girl reappeared, smiled at Celeste, and pulled on a velvet cord hanging from the ceiling. She waited less than ten seconds and pulled it again, more furiously this time, then looked at a side door expectantly. She looked back at Celeste and smiled again, brushed the front of her gown, then reached for the cord again when the side door burst open and a young man, brightly dressed, came through. He exchanged a few words that Celeste couldn't understand with the girl, who at one point clearly emphasized "Foscari". The young man looked from Celeste to

Marko, clearly unimpressed, and walked through yet another side door. "*He will take you to your suite, my lady.*"

Marko watched the exchange with wonderment. Clearly Celeste's name meant something to the staff of the hotel—though it wasn't like any hotel he had been to before. A young man, who couldn't be more than fourteen, came in and the girl at the desk directed him to take *Lady Foscari* and her 'footman' to a room she specified on the second floor.

Marko was unsure how he liked being a footman, though had to admit he wasn't sure what it involved. Visions of starchy shirts, fussy uniforms, and dome-covered dinner plates came to mind. But he would stay quiet if it got them a meal and somewhere to sleep.

By the time they reached the top of the stairs, Marko was dizzy. He could feel the day's efforts and lack of decent food in his gut. They followed their guide down a short, carpeted hallway where he took out a key and opened a door, then unceremoniously ushered them through it.

The room was not large; about the size of the lobby, but nicely decorated. A table and two chairs, and a small sofa that looked more decorative than comfortable, graced the room's center. A door, set in the back wall, must have led to the bedroom. Celeste said, "*Grazie. Per favore, bussa prima di entrare con il cibo,*" and, with a wave of her hand sent him away. The boy looked at Marko, and Marko returned his look with a shrug. Without a word the boy left, closing the door behind him.

After a few moments Celeste seemed to deflate, as if setting down a great burden. "Oh, Marko, that was... stressful."

He moved across the room to where she stood, reached out, and held her to him. "Can you tell me what happened? I probably understand more Italian than I let on, but a lot of things went on down there that I couldn't follow. What's up with their reaction to your name?"

Celeste pulled away from him and went to sit on the little sofa. Marko sat next to her, glad to finally rest, but already missing the warmth of her body against his. She looked at him. Exhaustion showed in her green eyes. "You're aware that my family is one of wealth, and that wealth has some history, correct?"

"Well, yes, both of our families are. But I've never seen someone react like that to my mother saying 'I'm Adrijana Horvat'. What is so amazing about your name?"

Celeste took a deep breath and let it out. "My family is old, and has very deep roots in this part of the world. A thousand years ago, or at least a thousand years before our time—Marko, I have no idea *when* we are here—my family was very prominent in this region. One of them was a Doge of Venice, which is like saying President."

Marko could see that, like him, she had come to accept that they, or at least one of them, was not dreaming. "So I gambled," she went on. "I thought that if I gave the girl my full name and got no reaction, then nothing would be lost. But if she reacted one way or the other, it would tell us something about the situation here. And it seems the gamble paid off. We are being treated very well. But to put on an act as an entitled debutante who expects to get what she wants because of who she is, *that* is nerve wracking."

Marko looked around the room. "We are, it seems, being well treated." With effort, he got up from the sofa and went to what appeared to be the bedroom door. Beyond it, a bedroom with a large, comfortable-looking bed, a large cabinet or wardrobe, and other standard-seeming bedroom furniture. The one oddity looked like a large wooden chair with an ornate metal thing in the center of the seat with a handle. Marko lifted the handle and looked into what appeared to be a chamber pot—no indoor plumbing, then. What appeared to be a dressing table held a basin, and a pitcher of water next to it.

A set of double doors opened onto a small balcony, large enough to stand on but not much more. It was no more than half a meter deep, only as wide as the doors, with a simple iron rail and little in the way of ornament or decoration. But it afforded a view of the harbor where Marko could see a set of docks packed with small boats, tied up and secured for the night.

To his left, Marko could just make out the tall masts of cargo ships tied at what must be the commercial port for the city. The sounds of dockworkers shouting to one another floated on the night air.

Marko heard voices from below and looked down to see a courtyard lit by open flames in pole-mounted iron baskets. The smoke smelled acrid, like burning petroleum, probably coal. Whatever it was irritated his sinuses.

He watched people standing in small groups on the patio, drinks in hand, pontificating on this thing or that. It could have been any one of his mother's garden parties, except that everyone was over-dressed for the warm evening in heavy capes, long shirts, or—in the case of the women—long gowns, all brightly colored.

Everyone wore some sort of hat or headdress, with many of the women covering their hair entirely. Marko looked down at his own attire, a button-down broadcloth shirt, shorts with large pockets on the sides, and vat-grown leather boots. Celeste was right to think that people here would be shocked at the sight of them, though he didn't have the faintest idea what to do about it.

He couldn't take the smoke any more, and retreated inside and closed the doors. He turned to find Celeste watching him. "What do you see?" she asked.

"People below having drinks and talking, just like you would see back home." He paused for a minute, wistful at the idea of being back in Rovinj, drinking beer with friends. "You were right about the clothing," he told her. "They have... very elaborate plumage." She smiled at his small witticism, and his heart beat a bit faster for her approval.

"I have an idea about how we can..." She was interrupted by a firm knock at the door. She looked startled, then waved him out of the bedroom. She followed and closed the doors behind them, then sat on the small sofa, upright with her back straight, and pointed furtively at the door.

Taking his cue, Marko opened the door to find the boy from earlier carrying a tray covered with a cloth, and behind him another boy a few years older carrying a larger tray, also covered.

In Croatian, the boy said, *"Dinner for the lady."* Marko nodded and stepped aside to let them in. He continued to hold the door while they set the large tray on the table and the smaller one on one of the chairs. As they were leaving, the older boy turned to face Celeste and gave a brief bow, then looked at the younger boy and urged him to do the same.

"Grazie." said Celeste, and waved dismissively toward the door.

As the boys passed Marko, they both looked at him. In Croatian, he said, *"Thank you, boys. Have a good evening."* They ogled at him, as if confused by what he said, but left without a word.

He secured the door and turned to look at Celeste. Both of them moved quickly to the table. Marko pulled the cover off the tray with a bit of a flourish. Hastily prepared, there was a small wheel of soft cheese, a loaf of bread, a bowl of nuts, and a piece of roasted meat, sliced and laid over. A ramekin held what appeared to be a sauce of some sort. Two plates held cloth napkins that were wrapped around crude-looking flatware.

Marko pulled the cover off of the smaller tray where he found a small pitcher of wine, two mismatched glasses, a large bunch of grapes, and a pomegranate, broken into segments. Marko examined the glasses. One was fine cut crystal, the other poorly made with chips around its rim. He was pretty sure he knew which one was meant for him. He picked up the pitcher of wine and started to pour, then reconsidered and put it back down. "There's a pitcher of water in the bedroom. We should drink that instead."

"What about dysentery?" she asked.

A vision of the two of them fighting for a place on the bucket-chair in the next room came to mind. He poured a small measure of wine into one of the glasses and tasted it, then said, "This is pretty potent stuff. Good, too, for that matter. If we dilute it with a little water, the alcohol will kill the bugs, and we won't end up further dehydrating ourselves."

She looked at him, blinking. "Whatever, I'm too tired to think about it. You figure it out, I'm going to eat."

It didn't take them long to devour everything that was delivered. Whether they were hungry or the quality of the food was very high, Marko couldn't remember tasting anything better.

They both paused when it came to the meat. Marko prodded at it with his two-pronged fork, then picked up a piece and sniffed it. He'd eaten lamb and goat a few times in his life, and plenty of fish. But animal meat as a primary staple food went away in the late twenty first or early twenty second century as vat-grown proteins, broad adoption of Vegetarianism, and general acceptance of sustainability as a way of life became the norm rather than the exception. Meat from a slaughtered animal, at least for non-agricultural Europeans, was expensive enough that most people went their entire lives without eating it. Marko, and presumably Celeste, were served it on a few occasions, but not many. He put the piece of meat in his mouth and chewed it some. It had a rich flavor, not quite spicy, and slightly metallic. He swallowed and said, "It's good, though I'm not sure what it is." Celeste tentatively took a piece, tasted it, then ate two more pieces before leaving the rest without a word.

They ended up drinking half the pitcher of wine, diluting the rest with water from the wash pitcher, and drinking all of the blend. By the end of the meal they were both full, but not even a mouse could have found a meal's worth of crumbs among the leavings.

Marko busied himself stacking the trays neatly with the plates, pitcher, and glasses arranged on top for easy carry. He folded the napkins and tucked them between the glasses to keep them from breaking one another, and set the whole assembly on the table. If he was going to be seen as a footman, he might as well play the part.

By the time he finished, Celeste was gone. He looked through the bedroom doorway to find her curled up on the bed, soundly asleep, fully clothed except her boots, which were randomly arrayed on the floor. He lifted the edge of the quilt and drew it over her, careful not to cover her face. She didn't move save for the gentle rise and fall of her back as she breathed.

He retreated quietly to the front room and looked dubiously at the small sofa, really more like two chairs merged by a single, wide seat. There was no way he would fit. A fabric rug partly covered the wooden floor, but nothing that would offer any measure of comfort, even given his state of exhaustion.

Back in the bedroom, he opened the armoire. The hinge squeaked and he cringed. He looked at Celeste, but she slept on. He found an extra blanket, heavy wool and coarsely woven, though probably warm. After a moment's indecision, he took off his boots, tucked them under the chair, and laid on the bed next to Celeste. He pulled the wool blanket over his shoulder, laid his head on the pillow, which was lumpy and covered in rough fabric, and looked at the woman sleeping next to him. As he sunk into sleep himself, his last thoughts were of how beautiful she was; that he would do whatever it took to get her home safely.

Crash! Marko came awake and leapt from the bed, tangling himself in the blanket along the way. For a moment, he wasn't sure where he was. He looked around the room and the fog began to lift. Celeste stood on the other side of the bed, and looked confused herself.

Through the open bedroom door, a boy whom Marko might recognize from the night before if his head didn't hurt so much, stood staring back at him, a half-empty tray in his hands and a shocked look on his face. Through all the confusion, Marko's bladder threatened to erupt if it didn't get attention soon.

Still in a fog, Marko maneuvered around the end of the bed and through the doorway. The boy kept looking from Celeste to Marko with shock on his face. Marko pulled the door closed behind him. "What happened?" demanded Marko, then remembered himself and switched to Croatian. "*What happened?*" he asked, in what he hoped was a less angry-sounding tone.

"*I am sorry, sir, the tray was heavy. I was...*" From there, Marko couldn't make out what the boy said. He kept looking at the door as he rambled on, something to do with the kitchen and the late hour and lunch, but the language, clearly Croatian, was a dialect that Marko wasn't familiar with. It sounded... old.

The boy finished talking and stared at Marko, wide-eyed. Marko tried to review what the boy just said to see if there was a question he was supposed to answer, but couldn't figure out what it might be. The boy looked furtively at the bedroom door, then back to Marko.

"*What is the hour?*" Marko asked. Simple language seemed the best approach.

"*Half past ten.*" Marko tried to think about how long they were asleep, but his bladder's assault took too much of his concentration.

"*Thank you.*" he said. "*Clean that, take it and go. We will depart soon.*"

The boy nodded, and Marko made his way to the bedroom door, slightly hunched to relieve the strain in his abdomen. He knocked on the door, heard Celeste respond, went in, and closed the door behind him, leaving the boy to clean the mess and stare in wonder.

The room smelled like piss and sweat combined with a scent that Marko found familiar but fleeting. With the door closed, the only light came from the seam between the balcony doors. It showed Celeste at the wash basin attempting to mash down her curls, and the curls were winning the battle. She looked at him, red-rimmed eyes and blotchy face showing exhaustion.

Marko crossed the room and pulled the balcony doors open. Light and heat rushed in, nearly blinding him. Unable to ignore the issue any longer, he went to the chamber pot, lifted the lid, and was assaulted by the smell of urine, unctuous and raw. He emptied his bladder, fighting the urge to retch as a cloud of stench further assaulted his nostrils, distinctly aware of the amount of noise he made.

Finished, he put the lid back on the pot. Within moments, the morning breeze cleared the room, replacing the stench with the smell of food. He looked at Celeste sheepishly. "I'm sorry about that."

She shrugged her shoulders and made a pfft sound, as if his ill-mannered display didn't deserve consideration. Relieved in body and mind, he looked around the room and said with resignation. "So much for waking up from a dream."

She looked back at him and pressed her lips into a thin line. With a sigh, she said, "It seems my dream of this being a dream is instead a slow-paced nightmare."

They did their best to freshen up and look presentable, though it seemed to be a losing battle. From the balcony they looked down on the patio where a small handful of people were gathered. Celeste seemed to study them intently, though Marko couldn't see that they were doing anything more than talking to one another in voices too low to make out.

She turned to him and said, "We need to get underway. Gathering supplies is going to be a complicated bit of work." He looked at her quizzically, and she said, "We are in a world that is not our own. However we got here, and however long we have to stay, we must operate by this world's rules, which are not the ones we are used to." Her look softened. "Marko, my sweet boy, follow my lead."

He smiled at her ruefully. "Did Mata Hari have a sidekick?"

She smiled back. "I don't know who that is, but Daria Valenti does; a man named Hale." She winked at him. "She keeps him around for his good looks and ability to lift large, heavy objects."

Daria Valenti, a war hero in real life who went on to star in her own series of sensationalized action films full of intrigue, speed, and ass-kicking, indeed had a sidekick named Hale.

A huge man from central Africa, handsome with loads of sex appeal and strong as an elephant, he was about as smart as a box of hammers. Except when it came to fixing things, which he could do with next to nothing in an impossibly short amount of time. Marko loved the movies, at the same time hating the lack of adherence to reality. "Hale, huh? I hope you think I'm smarter than that."

"I might. But I'm going to need some testosterone on this adventure, wherever it takes us. So for a little while, set aside any ideas you have about what makes a man civilized; I think that will help." Marko thought about the things that made a man civilized, and couldn't find it in himself to set them aside. But he would follow her lead and see where it went.

Her lead took them out of the room and down the stairs. They encountered no one, but could hear sounds of activity from the kitchen below. In the lobby, they found the girl from the night before sitting at the same desk, writing something. She looked up as they came down the stairs. "*Good morning, Lady Foscari. Did you sleep well?*" The question, in Latin, seemed tinged with some subtext, but Marko couldn't make out what.

Celeste seemed oblivious to anything the girl might be suggesting, and replied cheerily, "*I did, yes. A welcome rest. Thank you, and thank you to your family.*" Marko listened at the edges of his comprehension of the language.

"*We are... pleased... to have you.*" Again, something was going on there. Had he and Celeste done something to offend the family that ran the house? Marko thought back to stacking the trays. He was trying to be helpful...

"*Young lady,*" said Celeste, though the girl was probably no younger than Celeste herself, "*my predicament requires that I find a clothier immediately.*" She looked down at herself and expressed disgust. "*I cannot be seen in public like this. The idea of going back onto the street, here in a civilized city, is terrible.*"

The girl paused for a minute, then seemed to surprise herself. She looked Celeste up and down and said, "*I have an idea, if you'll permit. Come, follow me.*"

She led Celeste to the foot of the stairs. Marko made to follow, and Celeste said, "You wait here." Feeling somewhat rebuffed at her brusque tone, he turned and sat in one of the side chairs, determined to be as patient as needed.

Celeste followed the girl up the stairs, past the second floor to the attic. A long central hallway contained several doors off of each side. Finishes in this part of the house were minimal, but the walls were plastered and the doorways were trimmed, albeit without decorative bits at the corners. At the end of the hall the girl opened a door and said, "This is my room. It is simple, but I have it to myself. My brothers share a room of the same size. I am sorry it is so... poor."

In the room, dark until the girl lit a lamp, a small bed, made neatly, with a nightstand next to it. There were a few chests arrayed here and there, a small table with a wash basin on it, and a chamber pot sitting on the floor with no supporting chair.

There were no windows, and if there were a fire with someone asleep in that bed, they would surely die before they could get out of the house, if they ever knew. "It is absolutely fine..." Celeste began, and then, appearing to catch herself, said, "Oh, my, I seem to have neglected to ask your name. What is it?"

The girl looked shocked, blushed, and said, "Petra. It is Petra, Lady Foscari."

"Well, Petra, if we are to be friends, you must call me by my given name. *Lady Foscari* is only for people I don't like yet. Please, call me Celeste. So, what is this idea of yours?"

The girl beamed. "Oh, yes... um... Celeste... I thought... if you wouldn't mind... I thought that some of my clothes might... might fit you and that you could wear them until... until you found something better."

This was just what Celeste hoped the girl would come up with. The solution seemed obvious, but it would have been untoward of Celeste to suggest it herself. She feigned surprise. "Oh, Petra, that's a wonderful idea."

She stepped back, took Petra by the shoulders at arms length and turned her toward the lamp, assessing her. Petra was a bit doughy, though not fat, and about three to five centimeters shorter than Celeste, but one should offset the other. "We are about the same size, though you have a bit more..." She gestured to Petra's breasts. "Your endowment is somewhat more rich than mine."

Petra blushed. "Yes, maybe. But... well, I hope what I have is better than..." She gestured to what Celeste wore. Celeste, for her part, looked appropriately demure. The shorts, a cotton-linen blend with a ripstop weave, were hand-tailored by a shop in Trieste. They were comfortable, with good pockets, and fit her perfectly, owing to the work of the tailor. Her blouse, from the same shop, a light cotton shirt of simple design that didn't cling too closely and make her sweat. Perfect summer wear.

Petra opened one of the chests and took out a gown. Bright pink, trimmed in yellow and white, it must have weighed two kilos. She laid it on the bed and went back to the chest, where she hauled out another gown, this one less garish in forest green with white embroidery trim. She held it forth to Celeste. "This one is too tight for me here." She gestured to her bust. "I was going to have it let out, but you can borrow it if you like. I mean, just until you get something that is more appropriate for someone like you."

Celeste cringed. *Someone like you.* She hated the idea that Petra thought of herself as less deserving than Celeste for no reason beyond being born into a particular station. It was clear that Petra's family was of at least some means. They owned the house, after all, which must include staff and other trappings. Not that any of that should matter, since to Celeste's thinking everyone was intrinsically of equal worth, no matter what their financial circumstances. The idea of social classes bothered her, even if she was forced to participate in the facade in some way at home.

"Let me try it. Do you have a chemise?" Petra went to another chest and pulled something out while Celeste undressed. When Petra turned around, she looked at Celeste and gasped. Celeste looked down, considered how her modern underwear must look, and scrambled for an explanation. Finally she said, "They are the latest thing in Paris" and put up her hands in a gesture of helplessness.

The chemise, really more of a shift dress, was long, with mid-length sleeves and made of cotton duck. Like the gown, it had a boat neck, with little in the way of taper at the waist. Celeste looked at it for a moment, then pulled it on over her head. Petra seemed to relax some now that the scandalous underwear was covered.

As Celeste struggled to get into the gown, Petra examined Celeste's discarded blouse. "The needlework on this blouse is like nothing I've ever seen. The detail is amazing. And the weave of this fabric... oh, how do they do that?"

Celeste previously prepared herself for this conversation, having surmised by observing the people on the patio that the Renaissance had begun. "The world is changing rapidly these last few years. My family is spread wide, and brings the best things they find back home with them. I have been very lucky."

Petra nodded, seeming to accept the explanation. "I wish I could afford something this nice. Of course, I don't know where I would wear it. It almost seems like a man's shirt, but fit to a woman's body. People would stare, I think."

"People would, and do. I can tell you from my experience here." Celeste paused, as if considering something. "You have been so kind to me, Petra, so I have a proposal. Since you are letting me borrow these clothes for long enough that I can get proper clothes, you can keep that blouse."

Petra, who was examining the buttons on the blouse's placket, lit up. "Really? You would do that? It must be so expensive."

The blouse had indeed been expensive, as blouses went, but not irreplacable. She could get the tailor to make another when she returned to Trieste. "You have been kind to me," she said. "There is no greater gift than kindness, and how can I repay that? The blouse is a small token of my gratitude."

Petra grinned and made a high-pitched noise, clutching the blouse to her chest. "Thank you Lady... er... Celeste. Thank you very much."

A few finishing touches were added to Celeste's outfit, including a wrap for her hair. When they were finished, Petra tucked her new prize blouse deep in one of the chests, blew the flame out of the lamp, and motioned Celeste out the door. Down in the lobby they found a large man staring, arms crossed, at Marko, who sat in a chair seeming to do his best to look nonchalant and unthreatening.

Petra looked between the men and said something cheerily to the large man. The man looked at Celeste, back to Marko, gave a clearly dissatisfied grunt, and walked through the doorway that led to the kitchen.

Marko stood and examined Celeste's new set of clothes. He nodded approvingly and smiled at Petra. "*Dobro,*" he said. It was one of about four Croatian words that Celeste knew, and meant 'good'. Petra beamed.

Celeste rolled her shorts up into a cylinder, her hand slate hidden in a closed pocket. She thrust them at Marko, who took them from her and put them away in his pack. To Petra she said, "Thank you again, my dear friend. I have but one more thing to ask you: could you direct me to a jeweler who would pay me a fair price for a necklace?"

Petra pooched out her lips and narrowed her eyes. "Go to Margolis the Jew. He is a fair man, though is gruff before noon. My mother buys pieces from him when she can afford it. Tell him that you were referred by Jurić House. Our name is not important, but it is not unknown."

Petra gave them directions and they were on their way. Celeste mentally checked the first item off of her list, then looked at Marko in his modern clothes and crossed out the checkmark in her mind. She couldn't afford to get ahead of herself.

After they left Jurić House, Celeste asked, "Who was that man?"

"The girl's father. He came out of the back, looked around for the girl, and then stared at me like I spit on his mother's grave. I pointed upstairs. He just stood there staring at me until you came back down."

"How do you know it was Petra's father?"

Marko reviewed the scene in his head. "When the girl... Petra? When she came down, she said 'hello Papa' and seemed to try and distract him away from us. What happened?"

"I have no idea, other than Petra lent me some of her clothes until I can get some of my own. She told me where to find the shop that made this dress, and said that they might be able to direct me to somewhere that..." Her voice caught, and she sniffed.

"What is it?" He stepped ahead slightly so he could see her face. Her eyes welled up with tears.

"Oh, Marko, it's terrible. That girl, who is the same as me in so many ways, thinks that I am her better because of my family name."

Marko pulled her close and she laid her head on his chest. He still struggled to accept that they were transported to what appeared to be medieval times. In truth, he and Celeste, and their families, were cognizant of the fact they were more fortunate than others. Wealth had, more than a century ago, brought them long life and good health.

Did this make them 'better' than those who lived short lives in poverty? In some aspects it did.

Since The Last War, people like them—called *Montis*, or *Montignet's Bastards* depending on perspective, after the scientist who developed the age-slowing treatment—were careful not to publicly admit to their undeniable wealth, and went out of their way to deny that it was anything worth talking about. Even in private, parents schooled their children to avoid thinking of themselves as better than those less fortunate. By the time Marko's parents were born, some forty years after the war's end, the sentiment was well-rehearsed enough that Marko and his peers actually believed what they were told.

Marko and Celeste became aware that people on the street were staring at them. Celeste pulled away from him, wiped her eyes, and brushed the front of her gown. "I'm sorry, I think I'm exhausted." She looked at the people around her, who stared as they walked past, and without acknowledging them at all, continued following Petra's directions.

Marko followed along dutifully. As he watched her, he thought about her emotional upset. He found it confusing that this strong, direct, assertive—and, if he was being honest with himself, somewhat vulgar—woman he was so enamored with could be so affected by being faced with something that was clearly known for hundreds of years.

He remembered a day he and his father were out fishing a few years ago. Seemingly out of the blue, in the way Karlo commonly did, his father said, "My son, the most important thing you have to understand about women is this: they aren't men." Marko asked what he meant by that, and Karlo went on to say, "You can't measure them by the same standards we men measure each other. Sometimes it works, but when you least expect it, you'll find that your yardstick doesn't have enough dimensions." Marko wasn't sure what a 'yardstick' was, but he took his father's meaning. This, it seemed, was one of those times.

With a little effort and a few more left turns than was necessary on the narrow, winding streets of Pula, they found Margolis' offices on the first floor of a building above a tin smith. From the bakery next door, the smell of fresh-baked bread filled Celeste's head and made her tummy growl in protest of missing breakfast.

In the hallway outside Margolis' shop, Celeste retrieved her shorts from Marko's pack and fished her necklace out of a zippered pocket. She took a moment to think about how Petra would have reacted upon seeing the zipper as a closure. Celeste couldn't remember when it was invented, but it must have been centuries after whatever time they were in. She stowed the shorts back in the pack and knocked on the office door.

They were greeted by a hawk-faced man in his middle years who peered at them suspiciously. In Italian, Celeste said, "*My name is Celestine Foscari. I am looking for a man named Margolis. I was referred here by the good people of Jurić House.*" The man stepped aside and waved them through the doorway, then closed the door behind them and retreated to a lounge chair where he took up reading a book, ignoring them.

The room was small, reminiscent of the lobby at Jurić House. A credenza created something of a barrier in front of the access to what appeared to be a workshop. The walls were nicely adorned, though not lavishly so, and beyond the chair occupied by the man who greeted them, there was no furniture.

From the workshop a voice called, in Latin, "*A few moments, please, and I will be at your service.*" Within a minute or so, a man appeared behind the credenza, smiling warmly. "*Hello, lady. How may I be of assistance?*" He looked from Celeste to Marko and back again, seeming to register Marko as there, but of no importance.

"*I have some jewelry that, due to circumstances, I am forced to sell. The good people at Jurić House, who were our hosts last night, recommended we speak with you.*" She held out her hand and showed him the necklace. He reached for it and she pulled back slightly, concerned that he would snatch it from her and bolt. He paused his reach and looked at her calmly, and she chastised herself for being worried. This was the man's place of business. She extended her hand further. *"My apologies, sir. I... I have recently had a poor experience and must admit to being... excitable."*

Margolis looked at her, examined her clothing, then looked at Marko. *"You said your name to my man there..."* He left the question unasked, but clearly expected an answer.

Celeste stood straight. *"My name is Celestine Maria Foscari, of the family Foscari, whom I presume a man of your... station and good business has heard of."*

Margolis looked at her, expression blank. *"And you mentioned 'circumstances', Lady Foscari. What are those?"*

Fear rose in Celeste's chest. Would there be trouble? This transaction was key to her plan to escape this place and return home. She took a deep breath, let it out, and looked at Margolis with what she hoped was a balance of righteousness and imploring. She gestured at Marko. *"We were sailing south along the coast from Trieste when there was a problem with our boat. We pulled to shore where my footman here was making repairs. We were set upon by brigands, and they took nearly everything we had. We walked into the night before we reached Pula, where the good people at Jurić House put us up for the night."* She gestured at her gown and expressed mild distaste. *"I am grateful for their hospitality in our... my time of need, but I am not used to wearing borrowed clothing, and we must have funds to return to Trieste."*

Margolis looked at Marko, and seemed to examine him closely, as if seeing him for the first time. *"Your... footman?"* His voice betrayed nothing, but it was clear to Celeste that her explanation was suspect.

Celeste raised her eyebrows. *"Sir, I have told you of my circumstances. You hold in your hand the last of my resources, a gift from my mother that I am less than pleased to part with. Will you purchase it, or will I be on my way?"*

He looked at her, at Marko, then over to the man in the chair. Celeste couldn't see the man's response, but there must have been no objection. Margolis pulled a small brass loupe from his pocket and examined the pendant. He looked at her, evidently shocked by what he saw, then returned to the loupe and examined the chain. *"Where did you get this?"*

"As I said, it was a gift from my mother. She brought it back from Paris, I believe, though I can't be sure." This part was true. Celeste's mother had been on a shopping excursion to Paris and returned with this small gift. Celeste liked it quite well, and wore it often, but it wasn't exactly a cherished treasure.

Margolis finished his examination and looked up. *"I have not seen such piercework before, and the gems are set in a manner I don't even understand. And the chain..."* He said something in a language she didn't understand, then peered at the chain again. He didn't seem to be doing a very good job of establishing his position to bargain.

She thought of the machine she'd seen in many jewelry shops that cranked out streams of gold chain exactly like that, tens of centimeters at a time. The necklace, at least the main body of it, was the shape of the crescent moon, 'C' for Celeste, a design printed in gold that could not be made by any hand. Tiny manufactured diamonds, each identical down to the molecular level save for the microscopic serial numbers embossed in one facet of each, graced the inner edge of the crescent. He looked up again. *"My lady, I can offer you a price of fifty ducati for this fine piece."* He handed the necklace back to her.

Ducati. She had no idea what one was worth, let alone fifty of them. One thing she did know, however, was that in negotiations, the key was to negotiate. She tried to appear as if she were considering options, and desperately wanted to confer with Marko. That, however, would pierce the lie she told, and that lie was thin enough to see through already. She took a breath and let it out. "*Sir, my circumstances are dire, however I cannot take less than eighty ducati for my necklace. As I said, it was a gift from my mother, and she will be displeased with me for selling it.*"

"*I will settle on sixty, my lady, but not one soldo more. It is a fair price.*" Margolis looked at Marko, as if convincing him might help the situation.

Celeste clicked her tongue to draw attention back to herself. "*If that is the price, then I suppose I must agree.*" She hoped that sixty *ducati* was enough to get them what they needed to return to the island and escape.

The man nodded, then went to the back room again. Within a few minutes, he returned with a small leather bag that both thumped and jingled when he dropped it on the counter. He gave Celeste a level look, which she returned. She carefully laid the necklace on the counter and reached for the bag. There was a sense of drama and intrigue in the air. The bag was surprisingly heavy.

"Let me take that," said Marko from behind her. She handed him the bag but kept her eyes on Margolis, who deftly swept the necklace into a drawer on his side of the credenza. From the corner of her eye, she could see Marko open the bag and examine its contents. Satisfied, he put the purse in his pocket. "You should get a receipt."

Celeste nodded, and requested Margolis write out a sales receipt. He looked momentarily surprised, but without pause took a sheet of paper from the cabinet, wrote some text on it, folded it in half, and handed it to Celeste with a smile. "*Thank you, my lady. I wish you luck in resolving your... 'circumstances.'*" His smile carried little in the way of warmth, though it did not seem ingenuine. The smile of a politician, Celeste thought.

The man in the chair put down his book, rose, and held the door for them as they left. Celeste's feeling of relief that they came away from the exchange without incident was nearly overwhelming. Her tummy rumbled again as they reached the street and the smell of the bakery assaulted her nose.

After the two young people left, Margolis looked at his man. "What do you think?"

A shrug. "They are definitely of good breeding, and she may be a Foscari. He looks like he's from here, but they spoke what sounded like English to each other. Neither of them has lived in hardship." He gestured toward the credenza. "What of the necklace?"

"It is an amazing piece. It will sell better in Venice. I know a man who will give me a hundred for it, perhaps more."

The men looked at each other with resignation and each returned to what they were doing. Some days, business brought curiosities. But business always continued.

At the bakery, Celeste tried to purchase a small loaf of bread and pay with the coins Margolis gave them. The old woman at the counter said that one coin was too much, and she did not have enough soldi or piccoli to make change. She ended up sending them away with the loaf and an admonition to pay when they had smaller coins.

In the street, Marko tore the bread in half and handed one portion to Celeste. It was warm inside, made from several grains, with a heady yeast smell. They both stuffed their faces happily, and the boiling sensation in Marko's stomach that bothered him all morning subsided.

People passing by stared at them until Celeste suggested that eating in the street like urchins was probably frowned upon, and anyway she was getting thirsty. Marko stowed the remainder of the bread in his pack and they went in search of a tea shop, where the boiled water used to make the tea would be safe to drink. They found no such place. They asked someone about it, and the person couldn't even understand what they were asking for. Tea, it seemed, had not come to this city yet.

Marko, familiar as he was with modern Pula, found it remarkably easy to navigate the streets of the medieval version. Little appeared to have changed, save for the lack of traffic and signage. The underlying hum of cars and lorries, the odd crackle of tires on pavement, the slamming of doors; all was gone, replaced with fresh-smelling air, people on foot, and the occasional cart drawn by a horse or mule. A waft of stench hit him as they passed near what must be a sewer vent and he revised his idea about the fresh-smelling air. But in general, the street layout was the same, and he found it easy to keep his bearings as he marveled at the sights around him.

Eventually they were able to break one of the ducat coins by purchasing a mezzetta of wine, about half a liter, and receive eighteen soldi in change, perhaps enough to pay the baker. The wine slaked their thirst and didn't taste like it was high enough in alcohol content to make them drunk. It was sweet and slightly sparkly, which was not to Marko's liking, but Celeste was cheered, and with that so was he.

Completing the transaction reminded Marko of the receipt the jeweler gave them. He fished it out of his pocket and looked at it. Written in Latin, it was a basic record of the sale of one collana for sixty of something marked with a symbol, which Marko presumed meant ducat. At the top of the document was a date. A cold shiver run through him as he read it.

Back on the street, away from other people, Marko pulled Celeste aside and thrust the receipt at her. "Look at this. Look at the date."

Celeste took the paper and looked it over. She saw the date. Her eyes went wide and she sucked in her breath. "This day, 25 June, 1381! My God, Marko, could it be true?"

"I think it's the only evidence we have, and everything we experience supports the idea that we are in the middle ages. I don't know what else to think."

Rattled, but with the initial shock of discovering the date behind them, they resolved to complete the next step in their plan to return home, which was to acquire appropriate clothing so they could stop drawing so much attention.

They found a tailor's shop, where Celeste, with translation aid from Marko, negotiated purchase of two sets of traveling clothes each, custom fit to measurements taken by the tailor, as well as some proper, unfitted clothing for Marko that he could take immediately. The dark brown pants, with blue trim down the sides of the legs, hung to mid-calf. Drawstrings held them around his waist and also tied just below his knees to create a blousing effect. The pants fit loosely, and were comfortable, though Marko felt silly wearing them, like someone in a street show for tourists.

A waist-length cape was added, along with a saggy hat to cover his curly hair, and the silly feeling was furthered. Marko drew the line when he was offered silk stockings. He preferred to keep his wool blend boot socks, even though they were desperately in need of washing.

Thinking of that reminded him of the persistent itch that took up residence in his groin from too much time wearing a swim brief and not bathing. How long was it since he showered before leaving on their excursion? It seemed like forever. Marko asked the tailor for an undergarment, and he added it to their list. The total order came to four ducati and would be ready by the next day.

They found a market, full of smells both rich and pungent, and for less than four soldi purchased a small wheel of cheese, some fruit, and another bottle of wine. And they returned to the bakery to pay their debt, which used up only one of the smaller coins they received in change at the market. They bought another loaf and added it to their stash, which seemed to please the old woman.

By this time it was late afternoon. Marko was tired, hungry, and reaching the limits of his ability to absorb and accept what he was experiencing. They walked half a kilometer or so to the harbor where they found a small park with a bench under a tree. There they sat and ate their belated lunch, drank the wine, which turned out to be terrible, and talked about what to do next. The smell of the sea air, salty with a hint of fish, was a pleasant change from the air deeper in the city, which had become cloying in the midday sun.

"This day is taking longer than I thought it would," said Celeste. "And I'm exhausted. Everything seems to take so much effort."

Marko nodded. "I'm exhausted too. I had hoped by now we would be on our way back to the island and on our way home. But even if we had a boat right now, if we were to sail back out there at this hour, by the time we got up to the cave, it would be after sunset and we run the risk of losing our way in the forest. Best to secure a boat today and leave in the morning."

After a moment she said, "The tailor will wonder where we went if we don't return, but I don't suppose that affects us any."

"If we successfully return home, I will count it as a win," said Marko. "If not, we can see the clothier tomorrow and retrieve our wardrobe, then work out what to do from there."

Celeste agreed, though it appeared to Marko as if she wasn't fully committed. His fathers words about measuring women came to mind again.

They rested some, then agreed to split up and meet back at Jurić House before sunset. Marko gave Celeste fifteen ducati and some soldi and kept the rest, forty ducati and some smaller change, for himself. He would need it to negotiate rental of a boat.

Celeste walked along the streets of Pula somewhat aimlessly. She had several hours before she needed to meet Marko, and little that needed doing before then. Mostly they agreed that he needed to be free of her so he could navigate the wharf and negotiate with its inhabitants without having to worry about her safety or how they were perceived together. So, taking a page from her mother's book, she decided to do some shopping.

She returned to the market where they purchased lunch and bought a woven basket that could be carried like a satchel. She filled it with miscellaneous items that they might need, including enough food to eat for dinner if it wasn't available at Jurić House. At one stall she found a leather-bound book of blank pages, closed with a large flap and tied with leather straps. The leather was carefully tooled with embossed detail that made it look like something a ship's captain would use to keep a diary. She paid ten soldi for it and four charcoal pencils.

She considered all she purchased that day and how much each item cost. By her reckoning, a single ducat was worth about a hundred Euros, give or take a bit, and sixty soldi made a ducat, so a single soldo was worth about one and two-thirds Euros. And there were evidently a dozen of the smaller coins, the piccoli, to a soldo. By those measures, six thousand Euros was a very good sum to get for a necklace that probably hadn't cost her mother more than two hundred.

She found a shop that served wine and settled into a seat near a glassless window with the shutters open to let in the breeze. She hadn't seen a glass window anywhere in the city, and wanted to look up when glass was invented.

Of course, without access to the Cloud, she couldn't look anything up. She wished her slate, apparently dead of any functionality and stowed in Marko's pack, was fully connected and working so she could research all the things she wanted to know about this place and these people. Hopefully by tomorrow it wouldn't be a factor any longer, and this would all just be a well-remembered adventure that she and Marko could tell their children.

She stopped herself. *Their* children. Somehow she concluded that, even after this adventure was over, she and Marko would be together. She gave that some thought.

In recent years, she told herself that she wouldn't have children until after age fifty, with a better target being age seventy. That would give her enough time to see the world, establish a career and retire from it, and then settle in to raising one or two children. Her parents would probably be gone by then, but her mother didn't appear to have much interest in grandchildren. It seemed losing their son in the war, then eventually having Celeste, made them happy for what they had and not wistful for something else.

Celeste thought of her mother's reaction to her daughter having gone missing, then pushed it out of her mind, determined to return before her mother experienced too much grief. She dwelled instead on the idea of being with Marko for fifty years or more. As Petra pointed out, he was handsome enough. He was tall, but not too tall; she could kiss him without stretching. And his broad shoulders and strong arms felt good when they were around her.

His green eyes were similar to hers. Through them, he looked at her with something she couldn't put a name on but recognized as special. They were beautiful, though she wasn't sure he'd appreciate that term.

She pressed her knees together, worried that anyone watching would see her flush and know what she was thinking, even if it was a wordless, foggy vision in her own head. In her mind, she wrapped herself around him, felt their bodies intertwine, felt him in ways she was yet to experience...

With effort she came back to herself, took the leather-bound book from her satchel, and retrieved a pencil with it. She laid the book on the table, unbound the straps, and opened it to the first page. With the pencil, she carefully drew letters in an artistic style that said "SHIP'S LOG FOR CAPTAIN MARKO HORVAT".

Pleased with her efforts, she turned to the second page and sketched the street scene she saw before her, noting at the bottom, "Pula, 25 June, 1381". She marveled for a moment at having written the date, which seemed to make their situation all the more real. On the third page, she began to write. Ten pages later the shadows were getting long and the evening air was cool. The sun would be down in an hour or so, and she needed to meet Marko.

She got a little lost on her way to Jurić House, but at one point spotted a landmark she remembered seeing the night before and turned down a dark street to get to where she could reliably navigate the rest of the way.

About halfway down the street, a voice too close behind her said something in a language she didn't understand. She spun around and found herself face to face with a man grinning at her with half-rotted teeth. His face was close enough to hers that she nearly retched from the stench of his breath. He said something else she couldn't understand and leaned even closer to her. She took a step back, and he grabbed her left arm hard enough that it hurt through the thick fabric of Petra's gown. Her eyes widened at the pain and so did his grin.

Fully understanding her situation, she pushed her left hand skyward, breaking the man's grip, then dropped her arm swiftly so that she held his right arm bound in her armpit. Simultaneously, her right hand dropped the satchel, formed a fist, and lashed out. The man dropped to his knees as Celeste leaned backward, lifting his arm with her body. There was a pop as his shoulder came out of its socket. The man screamed and she let go of his arm. He got to his feet and stumbled off into the looming shadows.

Celeste grabbed up the satchel and moved swiftly to the end of the alley where the setting sun shone down the perpendicular street. At the corner, she turned left and continued on the route to Jurić House, heart pounding as adrenaline coursed through her veins. From across the street she heard "Celeste!" It was Marko's voice. She turned to find him running toward her, short cape flying behind his shoulders. She rubbed her arm where it was sore from being grabbed.

He arrived and looked at her with a worried expression. "What happened? I heard someone cry in pain. It sounded like a man. I looked this direction, and after a few moments, you came out of that alley in a hurry."

She let out her breath, which she had evidently been holding. "Some disgusting asshole accosted me in that alley. I was stupid for going down it at this late hour. I dealt with it, though."

He looked at her quizzically. "What did you do?"

"Throat punch," she said decisively. "It's very effective. And he will be nursing a dislocated shoulder." She gestured at the skirt of the gown she was wearing. "He would have gotten worse if it weren't for this stupid-assed dress I'm wearing. It's heavy and hard to move in. Hopefully he thinks twice about attacking his next victim."

He stared at her, blinking. After a moment he began to shake, and then burst out laughing. *Why would he do that? What was he laughing at?* "What's so funny?" she demanded. "I could have been seriously hurt." She slugged him in the chest and he yelped, but continued laughing. She slugged him again for good measure.

"Fourteenth century Pula won't know what happened to them," he said as his mirth subsided. "We need to get you out of this little town before you develop some sort of legendary status." She pulled back to slug him again, and he put up his hands to defend himself. "Hey, stop that, I was just kidding!"

"You just be careful," she said, glaring at him, barely suppressing a smile, "or the only thing legendary around here is going to be the bruising I give you."

He took the satchel from her and they walked the rest of the way to Jurić House. Along the way, he told her that he'd secured a boat and it would be waiting for them in the morning. He didn't say anything more about it, but she presumed it would get them where they were going safely. She told him about her shopping trip, but omitted the part about buying the journal. She would surprise him with it as a gift when they returned home, a memento of their journey together.

They reached Jurić House as the sun disappeared behind the hill. Marko held the door for her, and she walked in to find Petra at her desk. "Lady Foscari! Um... Celeste, I mean. You have returned." Celeste couldn't tell if there was trepidation or relief in her voice, but decided not to dwell on the question.

"Yes, Petra, we have returned. Thank you for your recommendation of the jeweler Margolis. As you said, he treated us fairly."

"I am so glad. I see by your... Marko... that you were able to buy some clothing."

"Indeed we were," Celeste said. "We ordered some clothing that will be ready tomorrow. And we... I would like to pay you for the room last night and ask if we could stay one more night."

Petra looked nervous. "Um... my father... he... well, you see, my brother saw you sleeping in the same bed, and my father says that if you are not married, then he will not have you sleeping in our house. We are a good Christian family, and we have a reputation to maintain as a house of honor. I'm very sorry, Celeste, I truly am."

Celeste began to protest in an attempt to explain the situation. Maybe they should just leave without a word instead. In the end, she said, "Petra, please assure your father that nothing happened in that bedroom that either he or God would have disapproved. We were both exhausted, and there was no place for Marko to sleep besides the bed. We ate and slept, that's all. No dishonor has been brought to your house."

Petra looked at Marko, who stood near the door with his backpack and the satchel, not moving. Celeste undid the knot in the sash around her waist where she kept her stash of coins, fished out a handful of ducati, and asked, "How much do I owe you for the room and meal last night?"

Petra, who looked like she was about to cry, said, "One ducat will suffice, my lady."

Celeste handed her two gold coins and said, "Give these to your father with my apologies for any misunderstanding. I will not, however, apologize to him for something that did not happen."

Petra took the coins, looked at them, and said, "Please wait here just a moment." She turned and disappeared through the doorway to the kitchen. A few minutes later she returned and said, "Papa says that you can stay one more night, but Marko must sleep downstairs with the staff."

A wave of relief that they didn't have to go in search of other lodgings washed over her. She said, "Thank you, Petra," and handed her another coin. "This is for tonight's lodgings." Then she handed the girl yet another coin. "And this is for you, for suggesting we go to Margolis."

Petra's eyes got wide. "Oh, Celeste, no, I cannot, this is too much. My father is very generous, and gives me two ducati every equinox. It is more than I need for my purposes."

Four ducati a year as a salary, the equivalent of four hundred Euros if her estimation was correct, didn't seem sufficient for a young lady in the world even with the support of a family. She handed the girl three more coins and said, "Take these, my dear, and don't speak a word of it to your father. Women of our station should have resources of our own that do not come from the hand of a man."

Petra seemed about to faint, but to the girl's credit she kept her composure and, wide-eyed, said, "Thank you, my lady. Thank you." And then, as if she had forgotten something momentarily, said, "Oh, and dinner is being served in the dining room now. I can take you through if you like." She came out from behind the desk and led them through the double doors on the side of the room. She looked at Marko, then back to Celeste, and said with a note of apology, "Staff will be served in the kitchen when dinner service is over."

Celeste looked at Marko, who followed what was said. He nodded, and Celeste nodded at Petra. "Thank you, my dear, that will be fine."

Marko led Celeste along the wharf to a particular dock, then along the length of the dock to where the boat he secured the night before was tied. At around six meters, it was a single-masted skiff with a good-sized cargo box built into the center.

It was clear to Marko that the boat was well-constructed and not very old, though it was not fancy; a working boat, probably meant to carry passengers and small items along local waterways. Marko dropped the satchel full of provisions into the bottom of the boat near the tiller. "So what do you think?"

Celeste appeared unsure what to say. "Um... it's a nice boat? You know I don't know much about boats. Did you rent it?"

Marko smiled. "Actually, I bought it. I was looking for a boat to rent, saw a sign on this one saying it was for sale, and... well, it's ours."

Celeste's look turned to one of consternation. "Bought it? Whatever for? We're going home."

"We hope we're going home. I gave it a lot of thought, and what if we can't go home? What then?" Celeste started to protest, and he said, "I want to go home as much as you do, but we have no idea how we got here. If we can't go home, or we can't go home right away, we need resources. And if we can go home, we don't care if we leave a boat behind."

She looked at him for a moment, apparently chewing on what he said. "So, how much did you pay for it?"

"Thirty ducati; most of what I had. The man seemed pleased with the price, but not so much that I felt robbed. He started the negotiations at thirty-five."

They combined their remaining money—his remaining nine ducati with her seven, plus an insane number of soldi and whatever those smaller coins were. Marko couldn't remember the last time he'd handled cash money, let alone coins, prior to coming here. Management of them seemed like a nightmare when you could simply pay through the Cloud. He wondered what the value of their cache of wealth came to in the local economy.

The morning was still chilly as they got underway. Unlike the day before, Marko woke early due to the noise in the kitchen adjacent to where he slept in a bed shared with one of the cooks. The man snored for the first part of the night, but Marko didn't remember lying awake for long, and his bedmate was gone when he awoke to the sound of banging pots.

Breakfast consisted of a piece of salted fish, a fresh-from-the-oven biscuit of some sort, and an avocado. He imagined that Celeste was being served something a bit more upscale, but he was thankful for what he got and expressed it to Petra's father, who was also the head cook. The man still hadn't spoken to Marko, but accepted the thanks with a slight nod.

Before bed he had taken the opportunity to wash in a basin of warm water. Finally clean, he felt much better about life, but his state of being was nothing compared to how he would feel back in more civilized times. Medieval adventure stories failed to address things like bathing, defecating in buckets, and living day after day with one's own stink because laundry wasn't automated. And he was fairly certain he'd give his last ducat for a toothbrush.

Marko navigated around a cog that was sailing out of the harbor, deftly swinging the boom out, reefing the sail slightly with his hands, and managing the tiller with his hip. Celeste smiled as she watched him, and he smiled back at her, pleased to be performing well under her scrutiny.

As if she was reading his mind about the toothbrush, she dug in her satchel basket and retrieved what appeared to be a reasonable facsimile. He showed surprise, and she said, "I found a brush maker at the market. He had something similar as some sort of cleaning tool. I asked him to make me this, and he put it together while I waited. I tried it last night; the handle is a bit thick and uncomfortable to use, but it works."

He took it from her and stuck it in his mouth, and quickly returned to handling the sail. The bristles were stiff and, as she said, the handle was thick. He freed one hand and gave his teeth a much-needed scrub. He could taste blood in his mouth as the stiff bristles punctured his gums, but his teeth didn't feel fuzzy any more and, with the sun rising over the mountains, the day got just that much brighter.

It took about an hour to sail out of the harbor and up to Brijuni Island. Marko remembered a pier that extended out into the little bay next to the ruins of an olive press mill. He guided the boat around the point and noted that the mill was intact. No one seemed to be around, but it was clearly used regularly.

He pulled in next to the pier, secured the boom, and stepped out of the boat. He tied the stern to a cleat he found, then helped Celeste out of the boat with their luggage. He secured the bow and turned to find her standing right in front of him. Without warning, she threw her arms around him and kissed him full on the mouth.

Once his shock subsided, he returned her kiss and pulled her against him. After a long and pleasant moment she pulled away from him. He looked at her and smiled. They had been so busy lately that romance was the last thing on his mind. The last time their lips met was the night before they left the estate. "What was that for?" he asked.

"The way I figure it, you haven't kissed me in over nine hundred years. I thought it was about time."

They made their way through the forest along the path they took before. Had it only been two days? There was no evidence that anyone was there since. At the top, they found the way down the back of the hill and quickly found the way to the mouth of the cave.

Marko dug in his pack and took out a set of items he'd purchased the night before. He knelt down and struck flint against steel the way he was taught by the candle vendor, catching the spark on a piece of charred cloth. A few tries later, he developed a small flame at the edge of the cloth, and he used that to light a candle that he set into the base of a small tin lantern. "Well, aren't you resourceful?" Celeste asked as the lantern lit up the inside of the cave.

They found their way to the cave's end chamber. It was just as they left it; Marko could see where they fell to their knees in the sand, struggled to their feet, and found a wall to follow out of the darkness. His mind flashed back to their last visit here, to losing his just-eaten lunch on the floor of the cave.

He looked for its remains, but couldn't find any sign of them nor Celeste's. It was conceivable that the liquid evaporated, but he distinctly remembered letting loose half-digested chunks. He shuddered at the memory. "Well, here we are," he said. He held the lantern high and surveyed the walls of the cave. "Any idea how we get back home?"

Celeste touched the wall as the light went by where she was standing. "I have no idea. I was taking pictures of these symbols, then I tried to take a panoramic shot. I was standing here."

She went to where she was two days before and nine hundred years in the future. He held the light on her as she raised her hand as if she were holding her hand slate and turned completely around. "Do you feel anything? Does anything look different?"

He peered at the walls, looking for a change. He looked to see if the remains of their lunch reappeared. "Nothing."

They tried for more than an hour, perhaps two. Neither of them could perceive any change to their surroundings. "Maybe we went home and we don't even know it," Celeste offered. "Maybe we should go out of the cave and see."

Marko didn't have a better idea, so led the way up the dark tunnel to the outside. There, at the mouth of the cave, he could see where he knelt down and lit the lantern. They had made no progress at all.

Marko looked at Celeste and shook his head. Tears welled up in her eyes and she shook her head, denying what was clear to both of them. Marko reached out to her and she stepped into his arms.

They stood there, holding each other, for several minutes. Marko racked his brain trying to figure out a solution to their problem. Two days of struggle in an unfamiliar place, with the barest of resources to aid them, to find they hadn't succeeded was despairing. They had each other, but that was about it. What to do next?

He leaned back from her without letting go. "We should try to find someplace to stay on the island and come back to try again. Maybe it's a function of time or date or day of the week or something." She sniffled, then nodded. Her eyes were puffy and her cheek red from leaning against him. Somehow she seemed smaller than she was previously, as if she'd been slightly imploded. *Stress,* he thought. *I wonder how I must look to her.*

They returned to the boat, both dejected, and sailed around to where Marko remembered the Neptun and Istra hotels to be. Where the Neptun side had been, a manor house stood with a broad walkway between it and a seawall. Nothing stood where the Istra building was save a well-manicured garden.

A small skiff similar to the one Marko purchased was tied up at a dock, as well as a larger vessel similar to the cog they'd passed that morning. A stack of barrels, each about forty liters in size, stood on the sea wall where the dock connected to it, cargo ready to be loaded onto or that just came off of the ship.

Marko introduced himself at the manor house and said that he and his new bride were traveling from Split to Trieste and wanted to spend some time on Brijuni along the way. They wondered, he said, if there were any accommodations on the island.

The man seemed to struggle with the word *smještaj*, as if the concept was unfamiliar to him, but said that Marko should take it up with the lord of the manor who was in Pula for the day and would return by evening. Marko told him that they themselves had business in Pula and would return to ask by late afternoon.

He returned to the skiff and Celeste, and they sailed back to Pula. The harbor was crowded with boats large and small vying for seaway, trying not to collide. The breeze was strong, yet directionless, and exhausted sailors shouted epithets to one another in a variety of languages. Larger ships managed with crews on oars, abandoning the fickle wind all together.

They found a place to tie up, navigated the streets to the tailor's shop, and retrieved the clothing they'd ordered the day before. Celeste left Petra's gown with instructions that he should contact her and have her come in to have the dress mended and re-fit. Celeste left enough money with the man to cover the expenses, and told him that she would expect to see Petra wearing the dress at their next meeting, a meeting that Celeste privately hoped would never happen.

On the way back to the wharf, they shopped for some supplies that would make their stay on the island easier, including blankets, a tarp, a cookpot, two plates, some rudimentary flatware that looked like it ran the risk of more harm than good for its user, as well as several days' worth of food and wine.

Celeste suggested that they put together a gift basket for their prospective hosts, and they purchased two bottles of wine that the merchant insisted were worth the high price he was charging, as well as a wheel of good cheese and some oranges. She arranged the lot in a basket and wrapped the top in a piece of linen.

They purchased so much stuff that Marko needed to find a boy with a cart he could hire to help them get things back to the boat. The boy was overjoyed to receive a soldo for his troubles, and offered to hire on to the boat as first mate. Marko laughed at this and said it would have to wait until he owned a bigger boat, but when he did, the boy would be first in line for the job.

Celeste understood none of the conversation. Marko relayed it to her later, they both got a good laugh out of it. It was good to laugh with her, and after the disappointment of the morning, any measure of good feeling was welcome.

The purchases lightened their purse such that it contained fourteen ducati and six soldi, which to Marko was much easier to manage than the raft of coins they had at the start of the day. The provisions they purchased would last them several days on the island, and if necessary, they could return to Pula for more.

On their return to the island and the manor house, their gift basket was well received by the lord of the house, whose name was Lagorio. Marko couldn't make out if that was a first or last name, but the man answered to it either way. His wife was away on a visit to family near Genoa, and wouldn't be back for more than a month. He was Italian, or more specifically Genoese, though he was quick to point out that he accepted the rule of the Venetians and had no quarrel with them.

Marko just nodded, as if he understood completely, which he didn't. He and Celeste told a slightly different version of their story that left out enough specifics that it was unverifiable, yet peppered with bits of their stay at Jurić House so that if someone were to ask about them, there would be some perceived veracity to their tale.

Their wedding bands, they said, were lost to the thieves, a tidbit punctuated with a well-timed tear on Celeste's part. Marko marveled at her ability to play the part she was given. The slight language barrier helped sell their story, as did the wine.

Marko and Celeste stayed with Lagorio for most of a week, each day making the half-hour trek out to the cave and trying everything they could think of to get it to return them home. Celeste, who was brought up as a Christian, even tried praying, though Marko, who knew something of the scale of the universe, doubted that any God would have the time to even notice the struggles of a single being any more than Celeste noticed the blinking of a single electron among the billions of atoms that made up her body.

But he didn't tell any of this to her, respecting her faith or, more importantly, respecting her. They talked about it later and she said that she wasn't so much a devout Christian as someone who didn't discount the possibility that a God existed, and anyway, what could it hurt? He agreed that at this point, he'd try about anything to get them home.

Their ruse of being man and wife did not preclude them sharing a room. By the third night of their stay they were sufficiently accustomed to the rhythm of day and night that they didn't immediately pass out upon blowing out the candle that provided the only light in the room.

Marko laid in bed and watched Celeste disrobe down to the shift dress she had been sleeping in. Her long curls hung on her shoulders, and her eyes twinkled in the light of the candle. She smiled at him and blew out the candle, then crawled into bed next to him. After a moment, she said, "Marko?" He responded, but she didn't say anything more. He reached out his hand to lay it on her hip. It was bare. Nervously he moved his hand along the curve of her body until it bumped against her breast.

"You're... um... you're naked." He wanted to kick himself for stating something so obvious and unromantic.

"I am," she said softly and moved until the entire length of her body was against his. She radiated warmth, and her soft breath tickled the hairs on his chest as she breathed. Marko's entire body sung with energy like an iron beam struck by a hammer.

During their summer together, they were only able to spent a handful of weeks in each others' presence. As their love for one another grew, there had been moments of passion—a lot of kissing and heavy petting—but their parents were almost always nearby, and really neither of them was of a mind to rush headlong into anything too intimate. People like them, Montis, were schooled since birth to take the longer view of things and not spend themselves unwisely.

"We haven't really talked about this yet," he said nervously. "Not that I haven't wanted to, you know that. But we should…"

"Shhh," she said, and put her fingers against his lips. "I have an implant, and so pregnancy is not a concern. I love you, Marko, and I don't see that anything else matters right now."

His mind went blank, bereft of anything they might talk about. In a panic that the moment might pass, he shucked off his medieval briefs, pulled her on top of him, and gasped as her body settled to envelop him. Their lovemaking was energetic and all too brief, but satisfying for both of them.

They finished and she cuddled up against his side, tickling his chest hair again with her breath. "I suppose this means I've been promoted from footman," he said. She laughed, and after a few minutes they both fell into a deep and blissful sleep.

They made love every night for the rest of their stay, learning about each other as well as themselves. They talked late into the nights about their dreams and goals, all of which seemed more distant now. As their attempts to return home bore no fruit, the discussions turned to how they might make a life for themselves in the fourteenth century, and how they should conduct themselves with respect to what they knew from history.

They ate an early breakfast, said their goodbyes to Lagorio, and promised to return the following year. They were welcome any time, he said. His wife, he was certain, would love to meet them. Celeste pulled her cape close against the morning chill as they set sail. Marko, happy to be underway, was oblivious to the cold.

By late morning they were back where their adventure started, except there was no grand estate house facing south at the head of Gustinja Beach, no grand garden, meticulously cared for by gardeners under the watchful eye of his mother, nor the obelisk he and his father built to catch the sun's rays and cast a shadow on the sea wall you could use to tell time. None of it was there. Instead, there was nothing but forest as far as he could see. Marko wept, and hoped that Celeste didn't see him. Not that he minded that she might see him cry, but he didn't want his sorrow to drag her down any further.

By mid-morning they were outside Rovinj. The harbor there was crowded, with merchant and warships both maneuvering for position as they caught drafts of difficult wind around Sveta Katarina. Celeste waved at the sailors onboard the ships they passed, and they hooted and hollered in return. Sailors, Marko mused, didn't change much over the centuries.

The little boat, which turned out to be quite the speedster, cut through the low chop of the following sea as the wind carried them past Lim Bay, Novigrad, and ultimately around the point into the Gulf of Trieste. Shortly after they passed the point, the wind fell out of the sail and they were left with only a light breeze to carry them the rest of the way into Trieste. It was half the distance as from Rovinj to the point, but it took them about the same amount of time. They pulled into a commercial pier as the church bells rang five o'clock and asked directions for a safe place to moor. Twenty minutes later, boat secure, they were standing on the seafront promenade among the bustle of a busy port.

"Where to, Captain?" Celeste asked.

"This is your town, my dear."

She looked at him, agape. "This won't be my town for nine..." She dropped her voice and looked around furtively. "...nine hundred years. I'm hungry, and I imagine you are too. And while you may be comfortable spending hours, even days at sea in a little boat, my stomach is happy to be back on dry land, empty as it is."

He stared at her and pressed his lips together, thinking. He looked around, hoping to find some resource to help their situation. Trieste appeared to be much more compact than when he was last there. After a moment he spied what appeared to be a cafe that was setting up to serve dinner, down the promenade toward the main body of the small city. The sun was low in the sky, though it wouldn't set for hours yet. The light glinted off the glassware and table service silver, which suggested fine dining. Marko pointed. "There, I think. We should treat ourselves to a fine dinner and figure out our next move."

Celeste looked up and down at him, then at herself. "If we are going to have a fine dinner, we must be presentable and not look like we've just come from a day at sea, which we have. We should find a hotel, or whatever suffices for one here, get ourselves a room, and clean up. Then we can have dinner."

"I'll follow your lead, Admiral," he said. She gave him a slightly bemused look. "However, as you point out, I'm hungry." He unshouldered his pack and fished in it for a chunk of bread and a small bit of cheese left from lunch. He gave her part of each. "This will hold us off until we can get settled and eat properly." She took them with a smile of gratitude.

It took three tries to find a house with available accommodations. Trieste, even in the fourteenth century, had enough traffic that during the summer, rooms were scarce. It seemed that hotels, at least the way they knew them, hadn't been invented yet. There were, however, several houses like Jurić that welcomed travelers in return for a little coin. So on the third inquiry, an available room was found for the "newlywed" couple. It was a single room rather than a suite, but was more luxurious than the one provided by Petra's family. The bill for the night would be two ducati. Marko rummaged in their purse to pay the clerk. Their remaining money was running thin. "Perhaps that fine dinner will have to wait," he told Celeste. She took his meaning and nodded.

Thoughts of paying for things with a wave of his hand slate, with no regard to how much they cost or how they impacted a budget, crowded Marko's mind. He had never felt wasteful with money, but knew there was enough to live his life as he wanted with little or no impact to the revenues of the estate company. A few of his friends spent money lavishly, and he thought them foolish for it. At the same time, he never blinked at spending what amounted to a week's wages for a middle-class person on something like a decent hotel room. He stared at the coins in the purse and decided to re-frame his perspective on money and the way it was spent.

After a little discussion with the clerk, Marko discovered that meals were included with the price of the room, and that dinner would be served in the dining room within the hour. This made Marko feel better about the price they'd paid, though he reminded himself that the two nights they'd stayed with Petra's family included meals as well, so he shouldn't have been surprised.

They were shown to their room where they changed into a clean set of clothes. Celeste mused that she wished she had a mirror so she could be sure she looked presentable, and Marko assured her that she would be the most beautiful woman in the dining room. Her dubious look told him what she thought of his compliment, but she seemed to accept it gracefully.

"We have to figure something out," Marko said between bites of something delicious that he couldn't identify. He noted that all the food he'd eaten since stumbling into the past was packed with flavor. Everything, including the air they breathed, had a fresh briskness about it, attributable, he was sure, to the fact that the Industrial Era hadn't started yet and two centuries' worth of pumping the black poison of fossil fuels into the atmosphere was yet to come. "We have a handful of ducati left, but at two per night for our room, we'll be living in the boat within the week."

"Could we sell the boat?" Celeste asked.

"We could, but that only delays the inevitable. I'm not against doing it, but we need to have a plan for what to do with the funds we get. If we're stuck here, we need a long-term strategy."

She looked at him with a blank stare, clearly lost in thought. He waited patiently and continued to eat his meal. He discovered that he'd been subconsciously avoiding the small piece of pork loin at the side of the plate.

Steeling himself, he determined that if they were going to survive in this time, a concept in itself he still struggled with, they were going to have to eat like the locals. And if that meant meat, then so be it. He cut a piece, put it in his mouth, and began to chew, which seemed to break Celeste's reverie.

"We need jobs," she said. "That's both an easy and a difficult answer at the same time."

"Schrödinger would be proud," he said, thinking she would appreciate his wit.

Her stern look told him otherwise. "We need to be more careful than that. I realize that using English is something of a barrier to being overheard, or at least understood, and what is to us modern English is even a barrier to a native English speaker in this time, but we can't be too cavalier about throwing around anachronistic terms."

"It was just a joke," he said with a plaintive look.

Her eyes softened. "I'd hate to see that written on your tombstone."

He smirked. "Do they have those here? Tombstones?"

Her eyes twinkled; they were back to bantering. "Would you like to test the question?"

They continued their discussion through the rest of dinner and, in less hushed tones, late into the evening in the confines of their room. Much like the day on the shore of Brijuni Island, which seemed ever so long ago, they made a plan to marshal their resources and create a sustainable life for themselves, all the while continuing the hope that it would be short-lived.

The first order of business was to get a roof over their heads. The manor house was nice, and very comfortable, with staff to fill every need they could have, but two ducati per night was, as Marko pointed out, unsustainable.

With a little effort, they found that they could rent a small but comfortable apartment for an entire year for only twice what they paid for a single night in the manor house. A year seemed like an eternity to spend in the prison of time they were thrust into. But they had no idea when or how they could return home, and using more than half their remaining reserves for a year of shelter seemed like a prudent move. They saw the boat as an asset they could sell in an emergency, but it would work in their favor to have it more than the cash it would bring.

The apartment they rented was small, about forty square meters in two rooms, situated on a twisty back alley off of Via di Cavana. A market where they could find all of their daily needs was a short walk away. Their new abode was also conveniently close to the wharf where the boat was moored. At the princely sum of three soldi per month, it was an amount Marko hoped he could overcome by shuttling small cargoes and passengers around the gulf.

Celeste, who decided to take Marko's last name in order to avoid the risk of having to explain how she fit into the fourteenth century Foscari family tree, looked for work where she could apply her skills without resorting to menial service work, areas where she had no skills to offer.

Work was not immediately forthcoming, but the two hundred or so soldi that remained of the small fortune they'd begun with at Margolis' shop would hold them for several months if they were judicious in the way they spent it.

Marko found work with a small shipping company that was really more of a cooperative made up of boat owners who, as a group, paid a commission to a man who brokered deals for them. The commission was steep, but the work was steady, and the group worked well together. Marko noted that probably half the earnings of the sailors were spent at the tavern next to the office they worked from, and determined to save what he could so he and Celeste could formulate an escape back to their own time.

Marko was no stranger to the tavern, though. Many late evenings were spent drinking flagons of cheap beer and listening to stories about battles with the sea, bad clients, and the *Condottieri*, a general term for mercenary armies that were all that passed as government in some of the outland areas of Italy where the will of the Venetian Doge and the Council of Ten did not have as much pull. Marko didn't have any such stories, telling the group that he was too young to have such adventures. They all seemed to accept this, particularly as it made more room at the table for their own tales.

Within weeks, Marko was one of them. He worked to pick up the lingo of the trade as well as the local dialect, which endeared him to his new friends. Trieste was at the corner of the furthest reaches of the Holy Roman Empire, a stone's throw from the Austrian Empire border in one direction, and a day's walk to the Venetian border in the other. Everyone, it seemed, had their own native tongue, so Marko's poor grasp of the local language wasn't a surprise to anyone, and no one questioned it.

As a port city, Trieste was somewhat cosmopolitan, and their group of sailors included Italians, Croatians, a Greek, and a Turk. Besides Marko, a quiet and brooding Turk named Reis, was the newest member of the company, having only been a member since the previous year. Most of the rest were with the group for almost a decade, survived the Venetian war with Genoa, and were looking forward to happier times away from the action. The Gulf of Trieste, or Trst as the Croats and other Slavs called the city, provided shelter from the regional wars and political activity, as well as plenty of work for willing drayage sailors.

Early August, 1381 — It pains me to write the year, as if each time I write it I somehow fix myself more permanently to this place.

We have found ourselves an apartment in Trieste and settled in. My city is much smaller than... well, than I remember it. The edge of town is where Via Giosuè Carducci should be the main south-bound street through the center of town. Beyond that, grand estates, tiny hamlets, and farmland. The air is so fresh and clean, even in the heart of the small city, the breeze carries scents that are bright and complex.

Our apartment is on an alley, narrow and twisted, with buildings that loom over. I don't care to go out at night without Marko. I feel confident that I can defend myself, but there's no sense drawing attention.

The apartment is in the attic of the building, and has one tiny window that provides a bit of a view if you lean out slightly. The neighboring building is close, and Marko says that if there's an emergency, we should be able to jump over with no real danger. Here's hoping we don't have to find out.

I was surprised and pleased to find that the old Roman Amphitheater is nearby and actually in use! Signs indicate that a play runs two days per week, though it didn't say which days. That doesn't really matter, because I have no real idea what day it is today. I will keep watch for activity. In the meantime, I'm at least staying fit with the long climb up the stairs to our little home. It's cozy, but we're so exhausted most of the time, we find we don't care.

Early one evening, before most of the crew came in from their boats, Marko sat alone at a table trying to work out whether or not he and Celeste would run out of money before they were ready to return to Brijuni the following summer, which was the time they deemed it best to re-attempt a return home. Sailing made an income, but just barely, and if they hadn't been able to pre-pay the rent for the apartment when they arrived, they wouldn't be able to survive on what Marko made delivering cargo. Their savings would carry them through, he was sure, but not if there were any surprise expenses.

Lost in these thoughts, Marko didn't notice Grga, one of the company's founders, sit down across from him. "Tell me your story, Novy," he said, startling Marko from his reverie.

"What?" Marko asked, trying to gather himself. "I don't have any stories to tell."

"You sit here, dreaming of something. Maybe it is your beautiful wife, maybe it is of the girl you did not marry..."

"There is no girl..." Marko began to protest.

"Maybe you dream of the life you left behind when you came to Trst. But no matter, you dream of something. Tell me your story."

Marko fidgeted, uncomfortable with the questioning. He looked around, to see if anyone was listening. He turned back to Grga, leaned forward, and said, with as much conspiracy as he could muster, "I'm trying to think of a gift to get my wife for Christmas. Partridges and pear trees seem to be in short supply."

Grga narrowed his eyes and gave Marko a hard stare. "Christmas is months from now. Pears are easy to find, foolish boy. I know not what a 'partridge' is, but it sounds like something the French would have. Have you been to France?"

Marko felt penned in, and was sure Grga could see it in his face. "I've never been to France," Marko said. This was true, though he had traveled much further than that, to lands like North and South America, which Grga wouldn't know of. "I have traveled, though. You know this."

Grga leaned back, posing himself in a way that said he wasn't going to let the matter go until his curiosity was satisfied. Wordlessly, he stared at Marko.

Marko stared back at him, his mind scrambling to come up with something plausible; something with just enough truth to have the ring of it without giving Grga something that made him want to dig deeper. "Our marriage was not approved," he said finally. "Celeste and I... her family wanted... wanted someone else for her."

Marko didn't know what Celeste's family wanted for her, if anything in particular, in the relationship department. He needed to inject a hard truth into his tale without giving away too much. "We left together one afternoon, made our way to Pula, sold some jewelry for enough money to buy the boat, and escaped to Trieste, out of reach of the influence of our families." All of that, Marko mused, was the absolute truth.

Grga looked at Marko and, after a few moments, nodded. "Your families, they are... wealthy?" Marko's mind raced. Was Grga thinking to kidnap them? To hold them for a ransom that would never come? What would happen to them when their families couldn't be found to demand ransom?

Grga's look softened. "Don't fret, boy. You're one of us, no matter who you were before. All of us have a past; some of them better than others. But it's not just us that sees you, and you... well, you don't look like a citizen, let alone a *slab*."

They were speaking in their sailor's pidgin, a blend of Croatian, Italian, and a bit of some other Slavic language Marko didn't recognize. But Grga pointedly used the Croat word for "powerless" in reference to the general population of people at the bottom of society, made up of laborers, shopkeepers, and, to Grga's point, sailors. No one in this lower class had any political power at all; no vote, no access to anyone with a vote, and no wealth significant enough to influence anything in the political arena. To Marko's view, it was no wonder that the forthcoming millennium would be packed full of wars as those at the bottom learned to assert their own power.

"Remember," Grga concluded, "'distrust is the mother of safety.'"

If it was true that he and Celeste stuck out among the disenfranchised where they made their home, then they would need to be careful. But what could they do? For better or worse, their appearance was somewhat fixed. For them, with their altered genetics, it would be a century or more before wrinkles started to show on their faces, let alone the weathered, deep valleys that made up most of Grga's visage. Both of them had perfectly straight teeth, a standout feature that already drew some commentary from people. And what were they going to do when everyone around them started to grow old and the two of them remained youthful? In the twenty-third century, the average lifespan of an un-altered, middle-class person in Europe was around a century. For one of 'Montignet's Bastards,' apparent aging leveled out at around thirty-five or forty, and stayed that way for about a hundred and fifty years, when a slow decline started. Two hundred years after the technology that gave them extended life was discovered, many first-generation *Montis* were still alive, his uncle included, and their ultimate lifespan was not conclusively known.

Marko looked at Grga. The man had been staring at him for some time. "What do you suggest?" Marko asked.

The old sailor nodded slowly, contemplating his answer. "Do you know how to defend yourself?"

"I can hold my own in a fistfight," Marko said. Just the previous week, a minor brawl sprung up outside the tavern. It started with an epithet shouted at Reis, calling into question his parentage and insulting his religion.

Reis seemed determined to endure the abuse without response, but two of their company, who came from the tavern to see what the noise was about, stepped in, and within moments fists were flying. The rest of the company, Marko included, spilled from the tavern to defend their compatriots, and others from the street joined in. Marko, tall and strong among the brawlers, survived by throwing one solid punch after another. More often than not, his punches landed squarely, and he blocked most of what was thrown his way. Once someone stuck him from behind in the kidney, and his vision flashed white. He turned toward his attacker, blocked a second strike by grabbing the man's fist in his own large hand, and hammered on the man's wrist, which crumpled under the assault.

Within minutes the scene was over, and the sailors stood together with little to show in the way of wounds, which was more than could be said for their opponents, many of whom faded back into the shadows when it was clear who the victors would be.

"You're tall and strong, that's a certainty," Grga said. But then his look turned dark. "But what about when the stakes are higher?" From beneath his jacket, Grga drew a short rigging knife and laid it on the table between them. "Do you have the ballast to put a man down if they be a threat to your family?"

Marko stared at the knife. He imagined he and Celeste being set upon by men in dark cloaks in a darker alley and what he might do to respond. The thought of taking another person's life was abhorrent to him, but so was the idea of losing Celeste. On balance, he would choose to defend her to whatever extent necessary.

He smirked as he remembered Celeste's own alley encounter in Pula, and said, "I would fear for the man who laid hands on her whether I was there or not, as she's got an Italian-bred fire in her that can burn if mis-handled." Grga, who had met Celeste on one or two occasions, nodded in agreement.

"But if it came to it," Marko continued, "I imagine I would do what I had to, though I have to say that short of cutting rigging, splitting sacks of grain, and mangling my dinner, I don't know much about using one of those." He gestured to the knife on the table as if it were something he didn't want to be near. Did that one have someone's blood on it? More than one person's? Subconsciously he cringed away from the simple tool that suddenly took on a new, sinister aspect.

"I can teach you some, but not enough," Grga said. "I'm old, full of gristle and contempt, and lately I fend off attacks with a grim look and a growl. Talk to Enzo, though. He spent years as a mercenary in the employ of a lesser-known Condottiere before hearing the call of the sea. He'll show you where to stick a man for best effect, and how to fend off attacks when you're surrounded."

Marko grimaced, hoping he'd never have to use such skills. But skills were like money; better to have them and not need them than need them and not have them. He nodded in acceptance and, as if declaring the conversation over, Grga waved to the tavern maid for two more beers. Marko found himself wishing for something stronger, but brandy was the only thing he'd seen available in Trieste, and certainly not in this establishment.

Marko took Grga's advice and trained with Enzo through the Autumn months, mostly evenings and Sunday afternoons when the rest of the city was busy with other concerns. Celeste quietly remarked — not quite a complaint — that she hoped it was all worth it. Marko hoped it wouldn't be; that he would never find use for his newly-learned skills.

Marko's mind kept returning to that night at the tavern and wanting stronger spirits. He took contracts to move barrels of brandy from Monfalcone, a small city a short distance to the north across the Gulf, to Trieste, where he delivered them to a broker who sold them to various customers around the city.

According to the broker, a venerated winery in the hills above Monfalcone had a spring on its land that produced boiling hot water. About fifty years prior, the winery's owners hired engineers to direct the water through a building where they used it to heat copper vats of wine and capture the spirits as they left. The brandy they made wasn't the best to be had, but it was inexpensive, owing to the free heat used to make it, and the lack of troubles crossing any borders, as Monfalcone was also part of the Empire.

Through the broker, Marko arranged to make a trip to the winery. With a wink and a nod, the broker was vague in his communications about who would be coming, saying only that they were "a young couple of the world."

On Sunday, the seventh of October, which was Celeste's birthday, Marko surprised her with a "getaway" that might help relieve some of the stress they'd both built up since their arrival. He told her of the ruse, and they dipped into their dwindling savings to have some nice clothes made. Two days later, they collected their finery from the tailor and set off for a short sail up the coast.

They left the boat in care of the port master at Monfalcone, with whom Marko was familiar, and hired a driver to take them to the winery. They arrived in the evening, just as dinner was being served.

The family who owned the estate had evidently built up the importance of the unspecified couple, and set a formal dinner that involved invitations sent to two neighboring estates. After many weeks of boring monotony in Trieste, Marko and Celeste both were happy to play their parts, being doted upon by servants and eating fine food.

As luck would have it, at least from Marko's perspective, their visit coincided with grape harvest on several hectares of the vineyard. Paolo Cogliani, the winery owner, a smallish man with bright blue eyes, and his wife Cosima, a reserved woman of remarkable beauty, were overjoyed when Marko and Celeste both volunteered to help harvest the grapes.

Marko practiced his newfound knife skills to slice the clusters of grapes from the vines and drop them in a basket that he hauled to the cart waiting at the end of the row. His back was strong from weeks of muling cargo onto and off of his boat, and the work was easy. The afternoon sun was partially obscured by clouds, and made for a comfortable work environment. Marko was invigorated to be working at something new with Celeste at his side, and he grinned at her every time he passed her picking spot. Paolo chastised his two teenage sons for not working as hard as the guests, suggesting that they should work faster lest they find themselves picking grapes while everyone else was eating dinner.

The evening brought a much less resplendent dinner than the night before. Before the table was set, Marko asked Paolo for a tour of the distillery. The man happily complied, and proudly pointed out the engineering his family sponsored to make the system work three generations ago. He explained that they ran the distillery in the spring and early summer when the workload at the winery was at its lowest. It seemed that the amount of wine the winery could spare each year to make into brandy was small enough that they could distill it all and put it into barrels to age in those few weeks, and then they shut it down for the year.

"Does it work with beer?" Marko asked. Paolo looked like he didn't understand the question, which was possible since there was little in the way of language crossover for the two men. "Beer is like wine — it has spirit, at least a little" Marko said. "You should try to make some brandy from beer."

Later over dinner, having sampled aperitifs from the estate's private stock, Marko told Celeste of his "idea" to use the distillery to create something from the "poor spirit found in beer." After hearing that the distillery was shut down for most of the year, Celeste, with a much better command of proper Latin than Marko, said, "Your amazing distillery is an important asset of this estate. You are doing yourselves a disservice by not using it to its fullest potential. Buy wine from the neighbors and make brandy from that. And try my husband's idea to pull the spirits from beer. At worst, you've spilled some beer. At best, you have a new business."

Paolo and Cosima both stared at Celeste as if she had grown a new appendage right before their eyes. Paolo looked at Marko with raised eyebrows. By way of response, Marko said, "My wife, like yours, is both beautiful and smart." Or at least that's what he'd wanted to say. From the corner of his eye he saw Cosima blush slightly, so she at least took his meaning.

The next day they said their thanks and goodbyes and prepared to return to Trieste where, Marko said, he had important business to attend. Indeed, there was a weekly delivery contract for Saturday that he couldn't pass off to someone else in the company, and he needed to be back to undertake that.

As they were leaving, Marko offered to guarantee a purchase of the first three barrels of the "beer brandy" if Paolo could work out how to make it, aged at least three years and handled through the broker in Trieste. Paolo excitedly agreed, and the two men promised to stay in touch with one another via letter in the meantime, with Celeste promising to do the writing so that the letters were legible.

In the carriage on the way back to Monfalcone, Celeste asked Marko about the contract. "How do you intend to fulfill your end of the contract three years from now? Have you decided to settle into this life?"

"Hardly," Marko responded. "I will confer the deal to Antun, the broker in Trieste, and he will happily take it on, as his customers are always looking for new things. Three barrels will be broken up into two dozen kegs, and even if the stuff is terrible, the worst that will happen is that the buyers won't order any more. Antun will profit, Paolo will have a sale, and everyone but the customers will be happy. And if it turns out to be good? Everyone gets rich from the sale of something that will eventually be named 'whiskey.'"

Celeste nodded and smiled at him. "You are a sly devil, aren't you Mister Horvat?" Marko smiled back at her, happy to have her smiling at him. When they returned to their own time, he was going to ask her to marry him properly and consider a lifetime contract. She would argue, but he was sure he would persevere. That thought warmed him as much as the afternoon sun all the way back to Trieste.

Winter came and the cargo business dried up. The members of the company with larger boats still had work, but Marko's little runabout didn't have enough capacity for the few jobs that were out there. And the rough seas kept passenger traffic to a minimum, though there was the occasional intrepid traveler who was desperate to get somewhere immediately and willing to brave the sea spray coming over the gunwale to get to their destination on time. Since Marko was one of a few sailors regularly available, he got that work. But it wasn't enough to sustain he and Celeste, and their savings began to dwindle.

Celeste found a legal firm that would employ her for piecework writing copies of documents. Initially they balked at the idea of hiring a woman to do something that was, to them, clearly a man's work. But her demands that she be taken seriously led them to give her a document to work on (Marko thought in an effort to show her how poorly suited she was to the task). She returned it to them quickly and with a revision that showed how the original author had a conceptual inconsistency that would have brought the whole affair into question. They decided to retain her services after all, gender notwithstanding. Her income, though, wasn't sufficient to sustain them, and was certainly under market for the work she was doing. But it kept the wolves at bay when Marko couldn't work for several weeks at a time.

Christmas was celebrated for twelve days starting on December 25th and continuing into January, which to Marko and Celeste's surprise didn't include New Year's Eve. The new year, at least in this part of the world, was recognized on March 1. In neighboring countries, the new year was counted differently, and there wasn't even agreement on what year was the current one. One night at the tavern, someone quipped that at this time of year, someone could travel back in time by sailing across the sea. Hearing the man, Marko breathed a heavy sigh and went home for the night where he sulked until he went to bed.

The new year brought Spring, the weather warmed, and the world began to brighten. Marko's spirits brightened with the sunshine, though a look at their savings, kept in a small wooden box on the apartment's one shelf, cast a dark shadow. Five soldi were enough to sustain them for two months if they were careful, but even if the cargo trade picked up, there was no way they were going to be able to save enough to pay another year's rent in the fall.

They made a plan to leave Trieste and return to Brijuni on the first day of July, somewhat arbitrarily chosen, though they expected that by that date they would be entirely out of money. As it turned out, work picked up for Marko and he was able to add to their savings, so by the time their planned departure date came, they had twenty soldi to their name.

March 1, 1382 — New Year's Day. The calendar they use here is maddening. But Spring has arrived, so strange calendar or not, my outlook is brightening. July can't arrive soon enough!

While in Trieste, Celeste stayed in contact with Lagorio by letter, and developed a relationship with his wife, Agata, who seemed happy to have a letter-writing companion. The two lived close enough that letter exchange could happen within a matter of weeks with a reasonable chance of successful delivery both directions.

For her part, Celeste seemed to enjoy having someone with whom she could craft a relationship at a speed slow enough to avoid missteps of anachronistic revelations. She didn't socialize much with local people, and mentioned to Marko on more than one occasion that she had to be on guard the entire time she interacted with others. Marko, for his part, found it easiest to wall off the part of his mind that contained his old life, storing it safely in a mental box that could only be opened when they returned home.

In the last week of June, a day after the anniversary of he and Celeste's arrival in the fourteenth century, Marko found Grga, bought him a tankard of good ale, and told him that they were leaving. Grga didn't show even the slightest surprise at the news, as if he'd seen this coming for a long time. "Whatever pulls you away from us... from here... know that you've got a place to return, boy. You're always welcome in our port." Marko's rush of emotion must have showed on his face. Grga looked sternly at him and said, "Now don't do that, you're going to water this fine ale. You've chosen your tack, and you need to run with it. If the winds bring you back here, so be it. And if they carry you away to other lands, then we'll look for you and your little runabout in our travels, and drink with you in ports where we meet. It's the way of sailors, and the way of the sea."

Two nights later, with most of the company in port, six of them drank themselves into a stupor at a party in honor of their soon-departed member. Near midnight, Marko heard Celeste's voice asking where "Novy" was. He turned and watched her navigate her way through the dwindling crowd, bearing up to the leers and advances of the dock workers and other wharf rats who frequented the tavern.

She arrived at the table where he, Lucio, and Enzo sat. Marko was certain that his two companions were relying on the furniture to keep themselves upright, and considered whether he was in the same state. He grinned at Celeste, and motioned for her to sit on his knee. Without a word — how rude! — she turned and spoke to the serving girl, in a voice that seemed louder than necessary. She said she would be back in the morning to collect her husband if only someone made sure the men didn't drown in their collective piss during the night. Marko shakily raised his tankard and yelled, *"Husbandino! Hahahahaha!"* Lucio and Enzo joined in the laughter, though clearly laughing at him rather than with him. Celeste passed a soldo coin to the bar maid to seal the deal.

The next morning Marko awoke with a start as a bucket of sea water was thrown in his face. He found Celeste grinning at him as he tried to stand up, tripping over Lucio as he did. "What the hell?" he cried.

"You two looked so cute together, I thought to leave you," she said, taunting. "But I have need of your strong arms today, and my bed was cold last night, an experience I don't want to repeat. So get up, wash yourself, and let's get to moving." Through the throbbing pain in his head, Marko noted that Celeste had fluently adopted the local mishmash of languages used around the docks, and employed it here instead of English, which they used in their apartment and when they were speaking privately in public. He couldn't do more than notice, however, as the pain in his head limited his ability to think. Lucio, his back soaked as collateral damage from Celeste's assault, stirred, rolled over, and began to snore, never having woken up.

Marko spent the day, head throbbing, playing the part of a mule as Celeste prepared for their departure. They had intentionally not collected much in their small apartment, but "not much" was still more than they wanted to take with them on the boat. They fully intended to find a way to return home, and presumably would have nothing more than what was on their persons.

So they made a circuit of their neighborhood, donating this and that to the few acquaintances they'd made, mostly to families of the rest of Marko's company. In many cases, they collected departure gifts, and even though they ended up with a net reduction in possessions, they had more to pack in the boat than either of them wanted.

"I suppose that if we return home, Lagorio and Agata will find use for all this," Celeste said.

"*If* we return home..." Marko reflected. "You sound dubious."

"Oh, Marko, I don't want to. But what if we aren't able to return? What if we have to make a life here? I want desperately to go home. But if we find we can't, I fear that if I don't prepare myself, I'll be crushed."

He stared at her for a few moments and nodded with understanding. He had settled into a life here, and while he retained a strong desire to return home and see his family again, much of his vision of the future was centered on life with Celeste, and he could make a life wherever she was. He dreamed of a life for her that was less work than the one they'd been living for the last year, but in the end, life for him was with her, and the setting didn't matter much.

Two days later came time for their departure. The morning sun was warm, but the shadows were still cold as Grga and the others helped them haul their remaining goods to the boat. The loading was done and the cargo secured, and there were hugs all around and promises of meals in distant ports. When pressed, Marko and Celeste said they were going to attempt re-unification with their families near Split, which was at least partially true.

At the very end, the young couple were about to board their little boat and set off. Grga pulled a small package from his coat and handed it to Marko, who unwrapped it to find a water-filled compass, about the size of his hand.

"Reis had it made for you in Venice a month ago," Grga said. "His people are good with numbers, and it has some special decorations on it to help you with navigation." Grga's voice got thick, and he paused to clear his throat. "We hope it helps you find your way."

Marko stared at Grga and the rest of the men with confusion. "A month ago? I didn't tell you we were leaving until just last week."

"That may be so, boy, but it doesn't mean we didn't know."

Reis stepped up and pointed out a few features of the compass; a body made of silver, a large glass lens on the top, and a golden needle held in place by a pin in the center. Below the needle, lines were etched in black to show the cardinal directions. On the back of the piece the names of the company men was etched along with some script in what Marko presumed was Turkish. As Marko studied it, Reis said, "In our language, we have a saying that it is easy to say 'come' and difficult to say 'go'. We will all miss you, Marko."

Over his shoulder, Marko heard a snuffle from Celeste as his eyes welled with tears. He nodded, unable to find words to express his gratitude. Instead he put his arms around Reis in a hug, and the rest of the company joined them. Lucio reached out to Celeste and pulled her into the group, and they all stood there in silence for a few moments.

Eventually the group let go of one another, and Marko and Celeste boarded the boat and cast off. Celeste stood next to him at the stern and waved to the group, who watched as Marko guided the boat around the end of a pier between two large cargo ships, then caught the east wind and sped away.

Properus arrived at Lagorio's bay at dusk. Marko pulled alongside the dock, and a man approached in the fading light. Without introduction, he captured the boat's line and tied it firmly it to a cleat. Extending a hand to a clearly weary Celeste, he helped her disembark. The men worked quickly to secure the cargo box. The wind had blown steadily from the north all day, helping considerably to propel the small boat along, but Lagorio's dock was exposed and that same wind would not be their friend overnight.

Marko glanced at Celeste several times while he worked. She had taken off the bonnet that covered her hair, brushed the tangles out of it, then put the bonnet back. Marko couldn't fathom why, after a day at sea, that the condition of her hair under her bonnet was important, but he knew better than to ask. He and his anonymous helper finished their task and Marko said his thanks. Celeste ignored them both, and seemed focused on adjusting her clothing, presumably to make herself as presentable as possible after their journey. Marko looked down at himself, spotted a crumb of cheese in a fold of his vest, lodged there since his midday snack. He popped it in his mouth, brushed away any other crumbs that might be clinging to him, straightened his vest and shirt collar, and hung his pack over one shoulder. He was ready, and waited as patiently as he could for Celeste to finish.

He expected to be greeted at the front door by the man they had first met when they arrived from Pula a year ago. Try as he might, Marko couldn't remember the man's name, and really didn't know his position in the house. Instead, as he and Celeste approached the door, it burst open and a woman ran out, crying "You're here!" Celeste took a moment to collect herself as the woman rushed toward her with outstretched hands, tears welling in her eyes, paying no attention to Marko. Celeste seemed reinvigorated by her friend's enthusiasm.

"Agata, my friend," she breathed, reaching out to take Agata's hands. "It is so nice to finally meet you in person." The women fell into an easy conversation, chattering back and forth in a way that

Marko couldn't quite follow, though for him a bit of a language barrier impeded his comprehension, as well as Agata's accent. He smiled with amusement. It was certain that he had never seen Celeste so animated upon meeting someone for the first time.

Marko looked to Lagorio, who was standing in the doorway. The light from behind left his face in shadow, but Marko recognized him by his shape.

"Greetings," said Marko. When he and Celeste had been there the year prior, Marko's command of fourteenth century language had been minimal, and he and Lagorio communicated primarily through gestures and facial expressions.

"Greetings," said Lagorio. He gestured to the two women. "They seem to have met each other well." He stepped aside and said, "Come in, this wind is terrible." Indeed, Marko could feel his hat lifting off his neck and didn't want it to fly away.

Without a break in their furtive conversation, Agata took Celeste by the arm and guided her into the house. Marko followed, and shook Lagorio's hand in the entry hall.

"How was the trip?" Lagorio asked.

"For me, a fair day at sea," Marko responded. He gestured to Celeste. "For her, tiring I believe."

Dinner was finished, but their hosts, expecting their arrival, had directed the cook to make a tray for them. Agata presented them with the food in the parlor. The weary travelers looked at each other and smiled. Marko thought of the tray of strange foods delivered to them that night at Jurić House, a long year ago. So much had changed for them since.

Hungry from the day at sea, they happily consumed what Lagorio's cook provided. The two couples visited in the parlor and caught up on their respective adventures in the few weeks since Celeste and Agata last exchanged letters.

Agata had planned a garden party, inviting friends from other parts of the island and the mainland. She tried to pass it off as a coincidence that the party was scheduled for shortly after Marko and Celeste arrived, but it seemed clear that no such coincidence existed. Celeste appeared happy to hear of the party, and offered to help where she could. Marko could hear the strain in her voice, however. The happiness was a sham.

Later in their room, as they got ready for bed, her facade disappeared. "Marko, what do we do?"

"About what?"

"The party, of course. It's clear that Agata has planned this party around our stay here. The party is in three days, and I was hoping we would be through the cave and gone by that time."

Marko waited to respond. He wanted it to appear that he considered what she was saying, but in truth he had worked out his answer an hour ago. He knew this conversation was coming. "If, tomorrow or the next day, we go to the cave and are swept back home as we hope, then we will, indeed, miss the party. Lagorio and Agata will be concerned, of course, and there will probably be an island-wide search for us. But after a week or two, our disappearance will be chalked up to one more strange thing that occurs in the world, and a dozen years from now we will be a distant memory. If you like, when we get home, we can do some research and find if there are any historical references to people disappearing from Brijuni. I'm betting we won't be the only ones."

Celeste appeared to consider this. In a crestfallen tone, she said, "Oh, Agata will be so disappointed."

Later, as he drifted off to sleep, Marko recalled their conversation. In the year since they arrived here, he'd seen changes in Celeste. No longer the brash, determined, and capable woman he'd fallen in love with, she seemed to be regressing to become soft and unsure of herself.

He was reminded of his mother, who was very smart in her own way, but very concerned with what other people thought and put a lot of value on what were, to him, transient impacts of social challenges. His love for Celeste hadn't diminished, but he could see that she was changed. As sleep took him, he renewed his resolve to find a way to get her back home where she could become herself again.

The next day they asked the cook for a picnic lunch. They told their hosts, much to Lagorio and Agata's surprise, that they were going for an adventure. Celeste promised Agata that she would be available to help with the party planning the next day, but said after the previous day's sail she needed a bit of relaxation. Agata protested that she didn't understand how "adventure" and "relaxation" went together, but that she would expect them for dinner; that she could do without Celeste if she must.

It was late morning when they departed the manor house for the ruins. From there, they made their way along the path to the cave, where they could still see evidence of their passing the previous summer. It appeared that no one was there, or indeed at the ruins, since their arrival.

At the cave mouth, Marko took his fire starter kit and lamp from his pack, then deftly struck a spark and coaxed it into a flame as he had done hundreds of times since purchasing the kit from the Pula street vendor. He grabbed up the burning piece of cloth, lit the wick of the lantern, and snuffed out the tinder flame quickly to save the cloth for later. With the starter kit stowed and the lantern adjusted, they entered the cave and made their way to the back chamber.

Like the year before, they tried everything they could think of to induce the time-leaping function of the cave to take them home. They yelled, they danced, they prayed to a god they weren't sure existed, they touched the walls in various ways, and even at one point held each other and cried. Eventually they sat down and ate lunch, hoping that maybe full stomachs were a key. Nothing worked. After several hours, with the lantern oil running low, they gave up and retreated to the manor and tried not to sulk so that Lagorio and Agata didn't ask any questions.

As promised, Celeste helped Agata with party preparation, which mostly seemed to involve tasting and approving foods prepared by the cook. At Marko's request, Lagorio provided a tour of the olive groves and the rest of the estate.

Lagorio seemed to know every olive tree intimately as he inspected them for changes that might indicate disease or infestation. Marko's father owned two inspection bots, driven by artificial intelligence, that roamed the estate doing the work that Lagorio was doing now. The estate used the two inspection bots, a pair of olive harvesters, and a variety of other automated machinery to ensure the entire agricultural operation could be managed and operated by his father and a handful of knowledgeable people. This included the hectares of vertical farming industrial buildings, almost entirely automated, that churned out fresh greens, vegetables, and fruits to feed the region's populace.

Lagorio's operation, by contrast, employed a dozen or so farm workers all year, and dozens more during harvest season. The work was hard for everyone, including Lagorio. Marko listened in wonderment at Lagorio's description of the process overall, and thought of several ways that he could improve on the system even without advances in technology. He decided to discuss the matter with Celeste before saying anything.

The party turned out to be fun for both of them. Celeste seemed to be in her element, drifting from one conversation to another, mostly listening to gossip about the intrigue of the local upper class. Lagorio and Agata's contemporaries were all people of means, but not high enough on the social food chain to be accepted at court on any but the most rare occasions.

When pressed, Marko and Celeste were coy about their backgrounds, with Celeste saying at one point that Marko was a part of a shipping company in Trieste, and he had an interest in a winery that made some intriguing advances in distillation, and oh, no, she couldn't reveal any secrets, but that they should watch for new, exciting spirits being available in the next few years. This set off a wave of speculation, and the more Celeste remained mum on the subject, the more interested they became. Later Celeste told Marko that she was somewhat certain that, if the whiskey experiment turned out well, there would be a pre-established market for the product by the time it started appearing in public houses. These sort of people, she said, liked nothing more than to have been "in the know" on a trend before it happened.

After the party, they made three more attempts at the cave, each with the same result. Lagorio and Agata were clearly trying to not ask questions, but also curious what the couple was doing day after day in the woods. By dinner on the evening of the third day after the party, Marko and Celeste decided that it was clear they were trapped in the fourteenth century and never going to get home. Marko told Lagorio and Agata that they were out searching in vain for a treasure they'd heard a story about.

Marko looked at them sheepishly, and they all laughed at the folly of the situation. Celeste, ever the diplomat, said, "But we came to realize that the true treasure of this island is the two of you and your fine home." Both Lagorio and Agata cooed at this, and said that they, too, found treasure in their new friends. Just then the servants came in with a dessert tray, and the whole subject of treasure was forgotten, replaced by lemon tarts and delicious soft cheese.

That night, tucked into their bed and awaiting sleep, Celeste asked, "What are we going to do?"

Marko's mind tumbled through all the things that question could mean. He recognized by now that if she didn't offer any preamble, then she meant their general situation. "I don't know," he said quietly. "I don't know what else we can try."

"I think we've tried what we can," she said. Then, with a bit of huskiness in her voice, "I don't think we'll ever return home."

He put his arm around her shoulder and pulled her close, then wrapped a leg over hers to maximize the intimacy of their contact. "I know what you mean, and I want to return to our own time too. But for me, home is wherever you are."

She was quiet for a moment. Marko could feel her tears running through the hair on his chest, and was determined not to move and disturb her reverie. At last she said, "Marko, we're broke. We have a handful of soldi left, but not enough to establish ourselves in a new city. If we return to Trieste, there will be questions. And rent is due there in a few short weeks."

"I know," he said. "And I've been thinking about that. I have an idea, but I don't want to say anything... don't want to get your hopes up... before I have a chance to think through it." She turned her head to look up at him, but said nothing. Eventually he could tell by her soft rumble and steady breathing that she was asleep. Long into the night he stared into the darkness and worked through a plan. Success would depend on a key factor, and if that didn't work out he didn't know what to do. But if it did...

The sun formed a barely-visible glow on the horizon when Marko woke Celeste. "We need to go before the house wakes up," he said.

"Go?" she asked, still half asleep. "Go where?"

"To the ruins of the manor. Come on." He hadn't slept at all. An hour before he had snuck down to the kitchen where he found enough food to make breakfast for them, which he laid out on a table in the corner of their room. "Here, eat something," he said excitedly. "Oh, I've never wished for coffee the way I do now. I've been awake all night."

She looked at him with a mix of concern and incredulity. "Awake all night? Marko, what's going on?"

His resolve to keep his plan a secret broke. "Last night at dinner, we told Lagorio and Agata that we had been hunting for treasure."

"It was a cover story, Marko... I... I think you need some sleep."

He saw her pained look but ignored it. "Cele, I haven't lost my mind, I swear. Hear me out. Do you remember the main beam in the study at our house... the manor on our estate, back home?" The word "home" had become overloaded in their conversations, and with no context and as tired as he was, he wanted to be clear. He worried that he was rambling. He took a breath. "When the estate house was constructed, the builder carved a very specific description... a story, maybe... of how the wealth necessary to purchase the land and construct the estate was found... buried treasure, just like in the movies... here on Brijuni. It was found hidden in a wall at the ruins of the Roman estate."

She stared at him, her head bobbing slightly as she tried to process what he was saying. Her look of concern barely abated. "So...?"

"So, we've seen that the estate isn't there. So maybe the treasure is."

She looked dubious. "You want to... what, take the treasure for ourselves? What will the person who builds the estate do then? I'm very uncomfortable doing things that have a major effect on the timeline we remember."

In his late night planning, Marko stumbled on an idea that he didn't want to share with her now for fear of losing her support and respect. Instead of revealing everything, he said, "Let's just go see if it's there. If it is, great, we decide what to do. If not, we make a plan for what to do instead."

She chewed thoughtfully on a piece of bread. Finally she said, "Promise me one thing."

"Anything, my dear."

"Promise me that if we go out there and find nothing, that we will make a serious plan to establish a home and live our lives, putting the past... or the future... behind us. But not before you get some sleep."

He reached out and took her hand. "I have some ideas about that, too. But yes. Sleep first, then planning. But for now, can we go?"

They got dressed. Marko put the remainder of the food in his pack and Celeste tidied up the bed. They moved quietly through the house, down the stairs, and out the garden door. Sounds came from the kitchen as they passed, but no one saw them leave.

The morning was cool, and they both pulled their cloaks around them as they walked the small road that ran between the olive groves and the pastures. Within fifteen minutes they were at the ruin. "So now what?" asked Celeste.

"The directions carved were very specific. Oddly so, as a matter of fact. Papa and I discussed it once. It said, 'One room remained with a roof, where wild animals sheltered. There, behind the third stone to the right of the hall door, a chest of riches. With it this estate was founded and this house constructed.'"

"That is very specific," Celeste said. The ruin was made up of several standing walls, unlike the twenty-third century remains that were little more than foundations no taller than ankle height. Here, some had weathered rafters that held tile roof sections, but only one room remained with a complete roof. A doorway faced the inlet, and a well-worn mosaic formed a patio that showed animal footprints in a layer of dust. The morning sun, still low in the sky, cast long shadows across the doorway. Seeing inside was impossible.

Marko knelt and opened his pack, took out his lantern, and brought it to life. He led the way through the door, holding the lantern high so it would light up the room. Something grunted as if it were startled awake and, before Marko could focus on it in the changing light, exited through a doorway on the opposite wall.

By the shadowy movement, it might be a large dog or juvenile bear. If it were a bear, he wished he'd gotten a good look at it. At home, bears were only seen in places like Canada and Siberia, though occasionally there were stories of one being spotted in some remote patch of forest in the lower latitudes. He reminded himself that bears were dangerous, and they were lucky that if they had disturbed one, it had gone away without trouble.

Marko motioned for Celeste to stay at the doorway as he moved around the room, his left hand holding the lantern high, and his right on the hilt of his knife, ready to draw. He saw Celeste pick up a stray stone and stand ready to offer defensive aid. The light danced across the ceiling and walls. He stumbled while trying to avoid a pile of fresh scat; the smell in the room was pungent enough to be distracting, but not enough to overwhelm. He was happy for the gentle breeze that blew from one doorway to the other. There didn't seem to be any other residents hiding in the dark corners.

Whatever the animal was they'd disturbed, it made a nest of sorts next to the doorway opposite the one he and Celeste used. With his boot, Marko pushed aside a pile of leaves and sticks to expose the third stone to the right of the door, like the instructions said.

He knelt to examine the stone and the light from the lantern drew close so it only illuminated the pocket between he and the wall. He heard Celeste approach behind him and felt her lean against him. "Is that it?" she asked.

"I guess so," Marko said. He prodded at the stone with his hand. It was as solid as any other might be, and showed no sign of being loose or being the door to a secret compartment. Marko looked at Celeste, who was still holding the rock she picked up. "Can I have that?"

He used the rock to knock on the stone in the wall that supposedly hid the treasure, then on the stones to the left and right of it. "This one definitely sounds different."

"Different how? Hollow?"

"Not exactly. Just... different." He knocked again, and a bit of mortar fell out of one of the seams. He picked it up and examined it. "This isn't right." He set down the rock and drew his knife, then stuck the blade tentatively into the gap left by the fallen mortar. It went in all the way to the hilt. As an experiment, he twisted the knife and pulled it against the section of mortar that remained in place. That, too, fell away. With growing excitement, he chipped away the rest of the mortar surrounding the stone.

After the mortar was cleared, Marko tried to put his fingers into the gaps on the left and right of the stone and attempt to pull it out of the wall. But his fingers were too large and he couldn't get a purchase.

"Here, let me try," Celeste offered. He traded places with her and held the lantern so they both could see. Settling herself on her haunches, she inserted her slender fingers into the gaps, squeezed the stone, and pulled, grunting with the effort. The stone came out of the wall, but only about half a centimeter. She rested a moment, then pulled again, gaining another half centimeter.

Marko set the lantern down, careful not to set the animal nest on fire. He leaned over Celeste's shoulder and grabbed onto the stone at the exposed corners, finally able to get a purchase. He looked at her, nodded, and said, "Ready?" She nodded in reply and he said, "Pull!" Together they drew the stone from the wall.

Marko was giddy with excitement, and it seemed to him that Celeste shared his anticipation, no matter how skeptical she'd seemed before. He grabbed the lantern and pulled it in front of the hole. They had to shove the stone further out of the way so they could lean over and peer into the void left by its removal. Less than an arm's length in, past dense cobwebs, they could see a dark shape.

Marko lifted the lantern and handed it to Celeste. "Here, hold this." She took it and leaned back, providing him room to reach into the space. After a moment of groping around, with the creepy feeling of cobwebs clinging to his hands, he got a grip on the object and pulled it out. Whatever it was weighed a lot, and dragging it out took significant effort.

By the meager light of the lantern, they could see a centimeter-thick layer of dust covering a box made of some metal that wasn't iron, half a meter long, and maybe twenty-five centimeters high and deep. A hasp was held closed by a single metal pin on a short chain; there was no lock.

Marko rapped on the metal of the box with the handle of his knife. It sounded thick. "Bronze, I think," said Celeste. Marko worked the pin loose from the hasp and lifted it free of the staple. He looked up at Celeste, whose face registered trepidation and excitement at the same time.

They nodded to each other, and Marko pulled on the hasp. The lid of the box opened just a crack and the hasp came free in Marko's hand. Frowning, he said, "The hinges must be corroded." He reached for his knife and wedged the blade between the lid and the body of the box, then pried until he feared he would snap the blade.

Steady pressure opened the lid far enough that Marko could get his fingers in the gap, and he returned his knife to its sheath, gripped the lid and base of the box, and pulled. The opening grew slowly as Marko strained against what must be centuries of corrosion. Suddenly the hinge gave way and the lid freed itself from service to the box and Marko's grip. "Ow!" said Marko, rubbing his hand. Numbness and pain fought for position in his fingers, and the back of his hand felt like it was bruised.

Celeste held the lantern high and leaned in. Marko also leaned over the box, and the two cracked their heads together. "Hey!" she cried, "Make room!"

They tried again. Light from the lantern glinted off of row upon row of what appeared to be gold coins arrayed in half the box. The other half of the box, separated from the coins by a divider, held leather pouches. Celeste set the lantern down gently on the rows of coins and picked out one of the pouches. It had a flap, but no drawstring or other closure. She tipped its contents into her hand, and let out a gasp as many-colored jewels tumbled out.

"Marko, this is incredible!" She sounded giddy.

He turned to face her and sat with his back against the wall, heart pounding with excitement. "So the legend is true."

"Apparently so. I have no idea how much all of this is worth, but if we take just one of these pouches of gems, we should be able to establish ourselves well enough, and the remainder can be put back into the wall to await the people who find it and build your house."

Marko took a deep breath. He'd been up half the night wrestling with what he was about to say, and now that the time was here, he was more frightened to say it than he was of anything he'd done in his life. He started slowly. "So, I've had a thought, and wanted to tell you, but didn't want to until we... well, until we were at this point. Knowing whether or not there was a treasure, I mean."

She looked at him, searching his face, her eyes glinting in the flickering light of the lantern. The morning sun shone through the doorway and made a bright pool of light behind her, but their location on the opposite side of the room was still dark. The lantern still provided the light they needed to see each other.

"So...?" she said.

"I know how this is going to sound, but hear me out. What if we're the ones who found the treasure, and we're the ones who built the estate?"

"What if we're... what?"

"Maybe it was us!" He was getting excited, and his voice was rising. He remembered himself, and returned to lower tones, though there was presumably no one around to hear them. "I know this sounds weird; I've been up all night thinking about it. And I know how it sounds, I really do. But what if we're the ones who, nine-hundred-odd years ago, found the treasure, bought the land, and built the estate?"

Her eyes blinked several times, and he could tell she was making a list of objections. "Who, then, carved the instructions in the beam?" she asked.

"Maybe it was us... me, probably, since I know what it says."

"And how do you know what it says?"

"I lived in that house my whole life; I've read it thousands of times."

"So you would know what to write..."

"Yes!" he said. He was finally getting through to her.

"That doesn't make sense." Maybe he wasn't.

"Us being here doesn't make sense, yet here we are." He was desperate to get through to her. "I know how this sounds; I know it sounds like the ravings of a lunatic. But what if it's true? What if there's a closed time loop, and we're trapped in it, and the only way out is to find the treasure and build the estate?"

"Closed time loop?"

"Yes."

"And you think if we find this treasure, and construct the estate, then we will somehow return home?" Her face told him everything he needed to know about what she thought of his proposal.

"Yes... well, maybe. I don't know, honestly, but it's a hope... a theory." He was losing ground, even in his own mind. Things had seemed so straightforward just a few hours ago. "What I do know is that we're broke, at the end of our ropes, and I don't have any other ideas. But here we are, and here's the treasure, and there's empty land where the estate is supposed to be..." He trailed off, unable to articulate the complexities of what his mind saw as the path forward. He really wanted coffee, but it would be hundreds of years before it became available.

"If I remember correctly, it was in Croatian," she said.

"What was? The carving? Yes, why do you ask?"

"Well, I don't know Croatian, so I wouldn't be able to tell, but did it sound like it was old Croatian like Grga speaks, or the more modern form that you speak?"

Marko recalled the words on the beam in his father's study, which served as the office for the estate's agricultural operation. "I... I'm not sure, why?"

"I'm not saying I believe your theory, but as you say, we're here, and that defies explanation too. So if the words on the beam were written using language that was modern in form, then maybe you wrote it. Of course, there's no way to really tell, but it would be something."

Marko thought hard about the verse on the beam. Nothing about it leaped out to him as being old or new or anything. It was just... Croatian. "I'm sorry, but I just don't know."

"It's fine, it was just an idea."

They sat in silence for several drawn-out moments. Finally Marko asked, "So what now?"

"I don't know," she said, sounding somewhat despondent. "Part of me feels like if we take the treasure and build the estate, then we're giving up all hope of ever returning home. That we're trapped here forever. And however much I was willing to consider the possibility it was true for practical purposes, I don't think I'm ready to give up hope just yet."

She paused for a moment, but he knew better than to think she was finished. His wait was rewarded as she continued. "On the other hand, I have a hard time reconciling that we take enough of this clearly vast treasure for ourselves, then stuff it back in the wall in hopes that someday someone will figure out how to find it. Paradox or not, I can't see how anyone would have known how to find this box without the instructions you followed to get here."

He was afraid to jump to conclusions, but they had to make a decision. He gestured toward the box. "So, you're agreed we should take the entire thing? That we should buy the land and build the estate?"

"I don't know that I would say 'agreed,' however I'm willing to concede that I don't have any other ideas, and your plan has... well, it has certain merits."

He nodded slowly, thinking through their next steps. His late night planning overlooked one big challenge: how were they supposed to take the treasure with them?

Celeste looked at Marko in the light of the lantern, which rested on the stacks of coins. Gently she poured the gems back into the pouch and placed it carefully in the box. She had an unfounded fear that at any moment the entire chest, with all its riches and promise of a secure future, would evaporate into a puff of smoke, the universe's way of giving them the middle finger. She noticed that her legs were going to sleep, and she needed desperately to stand up.

She did so and Marko followed suit. She shifted back and forth on feet that were an explosion of pins and needles. Marko tried to push the box with his foot. It only moved slightly under what appeared to be extreme effort on his part. The lantern flame wavered slightly in protest. "This is too heavy to carry all the way back to Lagorio's house in one go," he said.

Celeste thought about Lagorio and Agata and what their reaction might be to she and Marko arriving with a chest full of treasure. Would they claim ownership of it, taking it for themselves? Would they want a share? If she was honest with herself, did they deserve to claim ownership? She wasn't even clear on what constituted the limits of Lagorio's estate. Or, perhaps, the ruin was part of another estate on the island.

Then she thought of Marko's idea that they were the ones to build Marko's ancestral home. Leaving aside the complications of how they were led here to find the treasure, if they were the builders, then they clearly retained most or all of the treasure. But what if the decision they made here and now became the deciding factor to their success?

Thinking about it all made her head hurt. She paced in a small circle, trying to restore circulation to her legs and help her think. The hem of her skirt kept getting caught on the debris strewn around the floor, and she idly wished for pants, which were deemed inappropriate for women in this time. Marko stood still and watched her, evidently waiting for her to provide a solution to the dilemma of how to transport the treasure. Why was it suddenly her responsibility to come up with a plan?

"I think we should leave most of this here," she said as a preamble.

She paused for a moment to collect her thoughts and explain how they should proceed and Marko blurted, "You don't like my plan?"

"No... I mean yes... I... don't interrupt me!" she snapped, immediately regretting it. The pain in her legs subsided, and she was able to think more clearly. She took a breath, calmed herself, and said, "I think we should be cautious with showing the extent of the treasure to anyone, particularly someone who may have a claim to it."

"Like Lagorio and Agata," he said, sounding accusatory.

She felt like she had to defend herself, a position she didn't like to take with him. In their year together, trapped here in the fourteenth century, there was rarely an occasion to disagree. And when they did, they almost always worked through the problem with logic and respect for each other's views. There had only been one real fight, and afterward they talked about it... well, really she talked and Marko listened... and they concluded it was more from pent up stress than anything. It was a conclusion she appreciated. They were trapped here together. Both of them were fully capable of living independently, but neither wanted to endure this hardship alone.

As she paced back and forth, she noticed him just staring at her. It was infuriating. If only he would... she stopped herself. She took a deep breath. Something caught in her throat and made her cough. The air in here was thick. "Can we take this discussion outside? I need some air."

"Absolutely," he said. He picked up the lantern, stepped over the box, and reached out to take her arm. Together they walked through the wide doorway into the sun, which was fully up. She felt the sun on her face, took a deep breath of cool morning air, and was immediately refreshed.

"Oh, that's better." She turned to face him, but held his hand to maintain contact, so he would know she was with him rather than against him. "Marko, I'm not against your idea. In fact, as I said, I think it has merits. But if we haul this treasure back to Lagorio's and say, 'hey, look what we found!' there's a chance they will want some or all of it for themselves. After all, we're their guests, and this may or may not be their land."

Marko pursed his lips and nodded some, as if wrestling with what she was saying. "So what do you propose?" he asked.

"I think we should put the box back in the hole where we found it, go back to the house and say our goodbyes to Lagorio and Agata, then sail around to the cove here and collect the treasure."

"You don't think we should give them any of it?" he asked.

"I think this treasure is meant for you... for us, and always was. Once we convert it to useable money and get ourselves established, we can send them a grand gift. But I think we need to control and manage it. That's the only way we can be certain we don't have everything taken from us."

He said he agreed with her, which was a relief. They put the lid back on the box as best they could and, with a lot of effort, stuffed it back in the hole and slid the stone in behind it, then hid evidence of their excavation with leaves and sticks from the animal nest.

They arrived in Rovinj late that afternoon. The wind was with them all the way up the coast. Their little boat, which Celeste had christened *Properus*, a Latin word meaning 'agile' or 'speedy', made the trip in just under three hours, delivering them to Rovinj's crowded docks with plenty of daylight left.

Medieval Rovinj was different than the city she remembered. Early in the summer when they first met, Marko had taken her to dinner at a cute little cafe in the middle of the city. He told her how, over the centuries, the narrow seaway between an island and the mainland had been filled in, and that was the street in front of the restaurant. She hadn't been able to tell when they had walked along what had formerly been a strait, but there it was before her, packed with boats trying to make their way through, crossed by several small arched bridges and one large, flat one as wide as a freeway. Almost the entire town was crowded onto the island, with piers for the port jutting into the sea to the south. A wide boulevard arced along the curve of the hill that was topped by a large cathedral. A row of buildings, some stately and others simple, stood between the boulevard and the strait, as if to obscure the view from the mainland of things going on in the rest of the town. The smell of the sea blended with those of food cooking and fresh scents from mainland farms, carried on the gentle breeze.

The *Properus'* equipment included a strong pole used for close-quarters navigation among other boats and to push off of mud flats and gravel bars if the tide or a river current created a problem. On Brijuni, Marko used the pole, as well as some rope and a tarp to create a sling, mounted to the pole, that he and Celeste used to carry the heavy chest full of treasure from the ruin to the boat.

It had been all Celeste could do to hold up her end of the pole, though she did her best not to show any weakness to Marko. They wrestled their load over the side of the boat, with Marko waist-deep in water where Celeste, nearer the shore, was only in up to her ankles. They secured their prize as low and centered in the boat as they could, in case an unexpected wave threatened to tip the boat and capsize them. Now, at the docks of Rovinj, they realized that the sight of a man and a woman carrying a clearly heavy load on a pole through the streets would draw unwanted attention. They needed another solution.

After twenty minutes of discussion, they couldn't devise a plan for transporting the treasure that didn't have a high likelihood of getting them robbed. In the end, Marko suggested hiding the treasure chest low in the bottom of the boat. Already the hold was half full of their possessions, mostly clothing, mixed with the gifts they received in Trieste, all covered by a sturdy tarp. If the treasure were hidden below that, it seemed unlikely that anyone would think to dig under a bunch of modest personal possessions to look for riches. "Obfuscation is sometimes the best form of security," Marko said.

Celeste didn't like the idea of leaving their future unattended in a strange city where they didn't even have one friend. She was already frustrated enough with the lies they'd told Lagorio and Agata, people who had treated them with nothing but kindness.

During the sail up the coast, Marko told her that he had pocketed one of the bags of gems before hiding the box in the wall, and left it in their room at Lagorio's with a note apologizing for their abrupt departure, and a brief but vague explanation that they had, indeed, found a treasure. Celeste wasn't sure how she felt about that revelation, and was frustrated that he did it without talking to her. It seemed like the frustrations were just piling up. But what was done was done, and here they were in yet another situation where they were stuck without the right resources.

With the boat secure, they set out to find lodgings. They would need to find an apartment for long-term living as they had done in Trieste, however that would take more time than was left to them that evening, so short term accommodations would be required once again.

In Pula, they stumbled onto Jurić House purely by accident. In Trieste, at least, they knew what they were looking for, but struggled with making the best, most informed choice. Here in Rovinj, a much smaller and quieter city than Trieste, finding a place to stay turned out to be easy.

Marko and Celeste Horvat, of no title but clearly, by their clothing and manner, people of means, were welcomed at the manor house of the Novak family, Dalmatians who summered in Rovinj and wintered in Ragusa where it was much warmer. The family was in residence, but only arrived the week prior. The staff, who normally ran the house during the winter, had the look of people unused to being quite as active as they were now, and Celeste was sorry for them.

The Novaks were happy to entertain guests who were new to the city, and didn't ask for any payment during the Horvats' brief stay. Celeste conferred a few soldi to the beleaguered butler with instructions that he should disperse it among the staff, which allayed her guilt.

Celeste barely slept either of the nights they stayed with the Novaks, worried as she was about the unguarded riches aboard the *Properus*. As it turned out her fears, though certainly founded, were for naught. The boat went unmolested.

Marko found a jewel merchant who was willing to buy two of the gems for what seemed to be a fair price, which provided the couple with some operating cash. From that, they were able to secure a nicely furnished apartment on the island near the main bridge to the mainland and the harbor.

Other than the waterway and bridges where there once was (or would be) streets, Rovinj looked similar to what she remembered, with its terra cotta roofs, randomly-arrayed streets, and stone paving. Like Trieste, it had a certain rank smell that underlay everything; nothing like the fresh forest smells on Brijuni. She had grown used to the smell of Trieste, including that around the docks. Rovinj had its own smell, and she supposed she would get used to that, too. Learning these streets would take a while, though the island was small. Trieste certainly had its neighborhoods where streets ran at odd angles, but it was a wonder of urban planning compared to Rovinj.

After they secured the apartment, Marko hired a cart whose driver looked strong enough to help move the chest of riches, wrapped in a tarp and lashed to the pole, to their new home along with the rest of the household goods. The man had evidently asked about the mysterious heavy thing wrapped in the bundle, and Marko reportedly shrugged and told the man that it was something of Celeste's, and who could understand women's possessions anyway?

Initially annoyed at him for citing 'women's possessions' as if they were something to be marveled at like a mystery of the universe, she reminded herself that for the next seven hundred years or so, men really did think that way, and Marko was playing a part. At least she wanted to believe he was. She didn't want to think that his time in the fourteenth century, surrounded by the likes of Grga and the rest of the crew from the shipping company, made him regress to a pre-Enlightenment mentality. She resolved to keep an eye on things and address it with him if necessary.

Rovinj, for all its hustle and bustle as a busy shipyard city, didn't contain enough wealthy residents to have much in the way of high-end merchants who could turn their hoard of ancient coins into useable currency. And anyway, without a robust banking infrastructure, transactions all seemed to be in cash. The idea of managing a cache of coins the size of theirs for day-to-day usage was inconceivable.

By their count, there were ten thousand Roman coins, each about twenty millimeters in diameter and weighing in at around five grams. They were slightly larger than the ducat coins they got from Margolis, though it was hard to say what the gold content was, which would determine their ultimate value in an exchange.

Marko was intent on finding a way to secure the land that made up the estate, and engaged an attorney to make inquiries by letter.

Maddeningly, responses would take days or weeks, leaving him to pace around and fidget like some sort of caged animal.

"Hire an architect," Celeste suggested one day. "You know exactly how the building should look. Just describe it to him and have him design it."

Marko waited more than a minute before responding, appearing to work through the idea. Finally he said, "I took a design class in secondary school, which included a segment on architecture. I could probably make some drawings that would sufficiently convey what we want. I doubt there's any sort of permitting or inspection process here, so no planning commission to deal with..."

The following week, Marko was out when a pair of men arrived at the apartment with a drawing table he had ordered. Later that day, Marko returned with a satchel full of something he called vellum, which looked like parchment to her, blank paper, and pencils. He sat up to the table and started to draw, and for a week they barely spoke except at meal time.

Keeping up appearances as people of means meant that they needed to hire staff. Celeste hated the idea of having servants, but she needed help with the constant chores that went with having a household in a time without automation. Even in Trieste, she took their laundry to a washerwoman in the neighborhood. But lugging the pile of heavy clothing down the street twice a week, then lugging the clean clothes back, took a lot of effort.

And she was never much of a cook, which meant that their meals tended to be a bit monotonous. She did her best to vary their diet, but ended up rotating between the same dozen dishes or so, interspersing trips to local taverns or what passed as restaurants when she suspected Marko was getting bored. For his part, Marko never complained, but it was clear to her that he missed the widely varied meals prepared by the estate staff while he was growing up.

She hired a housekeeper to clean twice a week, and a cook to prepare meals six days per week. The cook was a matronly woman, forty-five years old named Blaga, with two grown children and a husband who worked in the shipyards. The extra money she would bring in would help ensure a comfortable retirement in ten years if, according to her, she kept the money secreted away and didn't let her husband drink it all.

She insisted that he was a good man who worked hard and was good to the children when they were growing up, but in recent years had found a taste for wine that seemed to take up every extra piccolo. Celeste resolved to pay Blaga a bonus at the end of her service if her work was good, a bonus that would ensure a good retirement for she and her husband. Or just for Blaga, if that were the way it was to work out.

The housekeeper, Sanja, came and went with little in the way of conversation during her two visits per week. She was very businesslike, and said only what was necessary to Celeste to complete her work. To Celeste's knowledge, Sanja never spoke a word to Marko, even when he said "hello" to her. This was a stark contrast to Blaga who, after a few weeks, treated Celeste and Marko as if they were her own family, though still used what passed for "sir" or "ma'am" in the local vernacular.

During their stay in Trieste, Celeste learned to speak Latin fluently, and picked up the pidgin of the docks readily enough, but she still struggled with the Slavic Croatian language that was primarily spoken here in Rovinj. She relied on Marko almost entirely for any but the most rudimentary conversations. The language was so different from either English or her native Italian that she couldn't seem to retain more than a few simple words. Blaga knew enough Latin that Celeste, with a little arm waving, could communicate effectively with her, and Sanja had little enough to say that language barriers didn't really matter. Still, Celeste resolved to find a tutor who could school her in what was evidently going to be the language of her new home when the land was acquired and Marko built the house.

> *Friday, October 4, 1382 — We had a nice dinner with the Novaks yesterday. They are leaving today for ~~Dubrovnik~~ Ragusa. The weather is still mild, but the cold will be here soon and I would like it if we were going with them. Marko is so caught up in planning the estate construction, there's no way I could convince him to leave.*

> *Lady Novak mentioned that my Trieste has finally closed an agreement with the Habsburgs for protection against Venice rather than remain free. There is so much pettiness here, with power brokers angling for every scrap of land, every resource, with the only end being to fill their own bottomless pockets lined with greed.*

> *Home seems ever further away, and returning there seems ever more unlikely.*

It was strange for Celeste to think that she was living what seemed to be a predestined life; that it was a foregone conclusion that she and Marko would buy a particular plot of land and build a particular house. What might happen if they deliberately tried to change something? She rejected the idea out of fear that, like the classic butterfly that caused a storm on the other side of the world with a flap of its wings, nine hundred years of time might amplify the smallest change into a situation where she and Marko had never met, or even where they had never existed.

What would happen if they made such a change? Would they blink out of existence? But then if they never existed, they wouldn't have arrived here, and therefore wouldn't be here to blink out. Trying to unwind it all brought her to the conclusion that they could only do what they could do and nothing more. No matter, she found the notion of being dragged along through life by some master plan she could only partly determine unsettling.

Marko evidently had similar thoughts, and arrived at similar conclusions. Over dinner one evening he said, "I thought about making some changes to the house that might make things easier for us here and now. But as I thought through the impact of the changes down the line, I realized that the house, as I remember it, is as perfect as it can be given that it has to survive a millennium of technological changes. I started to marvel at the foresight of the person who designed it, then remembered the situation and how it was me who did the designing of the house I remember, and then why I had the foresight I did... or do." He laughed just a little at his own folly, and his mirth made her feel better about their situation.

"At any rate," he went on, "it makes it faster to just draw what I remember than try to do any design work. I drew up a guide for the footings, kind of a cross-section of the perimeter walls, but I'll have to talk to a builder to get real information on their dimensions. My study of architecture was scholastic at best."

Celeste didn't know precisely what footings were, and couldn't offer any input. But the fact that he seemed happy with his efforts made her happy, and with that realization came the knowledge that she had lost the independence that was such an important part of her life.

In her youth, she was certain that having independence was a large component of having agency, the ability to make decisions for herself independent of input from anyone else. Now, after a year of marriage to Marko, whether officially recorded or not, she saw that she could have agency and still have interdependence with someone. It was a powerful revelation. Marko, still describing his efforts to design a house that, for him, already existed, was clearly oblivious to her bit of enlightenment.

A messenger arrived at the apartment door one day with a letter from Marko's land-seeking attorney. He had, it seemed, secured agreement to sell from the owner of the particular parcel of land Marko was after, that of the peninsula surrounding Gustinja Beach. One hundred *iugăr* were offered for two hundred ducats.

She asked what an *iugăr* was, and Marko said that he didn't know exactly, but that it was a unit of measurement for farm-scale land and holdings. One hundred *iugăr* was at least a large piece of land, though he didn't know how it compared to the ninety-three hectares of land that made up the estate he remembered.

Celeste crafted a formal letter of response in Latin accepting the price. Since the owner lived in Hvar, closure of the transaction took three weeks, a time frame that the attorney lauded as amazingly fast. Payment was conferred using the gemstones from the treasure, whose value was estimated by a jeweler in the acquaintance of the attorney. Celeste suggested they might be the victims of graft, but Marko was so anxious to get the transaction closed that he said he didn't want to make any waves.

The purchase left them with one bag of stones in addition to the as-yet-untouched ten thousand gold coins, which they were concerned about dipping into in case the appearance of large quantities of ancient gold coins in the small town of Rovinj attracted attention they didn't want.

The legal document, called a *carta*, arrived ten days later. It contained a description of the land area based on roads, standing stones, the seashore, and a swamp. Marko said he thought he knew approximately where the boundaries fell, but wanted to go see for himself.

The idea of camping in the wildland that would one day be the park-like setting of Marko's home, particularly where the word "swamp" was in the description, sounded like a bit more "roughing it" than Celeste wanted to deal with, so she sent him on alone, to return the following day.

The next day, instead of Marko, a messenger arrived with a letter saying that he would be a few days and that she shouldn't worry. She paid the young man, no more than twelve years old, two piccoli for his troubles. His face beamed at her, and he bowed several times as he retreated down the hallway, espousing what she presumed was thanks in what sounded like Croatian before turning to disappear down the stair.

Two days later Marko returned, face and arms covered in welts that looked like mosquito bites, only larger. According to him, he slept the first night on the boat, but not having a proper dock to which he could secure the *Properus*, no marina or cove to protect him from the open sea, and with waters too deep right offshore to set the aft anchor, he found himself tossed about so that he didn't really sleep.

The next night he slept on the beach, which was apparently comfortable enough and without incident, but the third night, in the same camp, he was attacked by some sort of fleas, and awoke to find himself covered in bites. On seeing his condition, Blaga left and returned with some smelly lotion which she admonished Marko to use liberally, leaving him looking like a refugee from a zombie movie, with swollen pustules covered in a chalky residue. But he reported that the itch subsided, and within a couple days the bite marks were healed, so late medieval medicine must have some efficacy to it.

"So, what did you discover?" asked Celeste as she applied the lotion to his arms and back.

"I found that we've purchased about half the property that made up the estate I remember. It makes for a good start, and probably over the next nine centuries some of the neighboring property will come available to whomever is managing the estate at the time. The main house site is well within the bounds, though it's much further to the beach than in our time, owing to lower sea levels."

"I've been giving some thought to that question," she said.

"Sea levels?"

"No, the question of who manages the estate when... well, I presume we're not going to live for nine hundred years. I'm not sure I'd even want to." She dipped her fingers in the small crock to get more lotion. It sure was smelly.

"Well, the estate is technically owned by a corporation that pays dividends to family members and selects operators as the previous ones retire. When my grandfather Jadran retired about forty years ago, after about seventy-five years managing the estate, the board chose my father to take over. My uncle Vlad had no interest in the agricultural aspects, though was elected to the board some years back. Since I'm an only child, father was hoping I would take an interest in the position myself and be nominated, presumably getting a hand-wave vote from the board. If we can't find a way to return to our home time, I presume the board would encourage my cousin Oscar to the post, though Papa probably won't retire for another fifty years or so, if then."

"You don't think your parents would choose to have another child?" Celeste asked. Her parents did after losing her brother. It seemed the logical conclusion.

Marko was quiet for several moments. Celeste could feel waves of emotion rolling through him, expressed in the slow contraction and release of his muscles. "I don't know," he said finally. "If we don't come back... if we don't return... I suppose they may choose to... to replace me."

Celeste could hear the pain in his voice. "Marko, sweetheart, they would never be able to 'replace' you, and I can't imagine either of your parents thinking that way. But your absence may... will create a void that they may feel the need to fill."

"I suppose so," he said finally. "And, depending on his or her ultimate life goals, they may take over management of the estate. Or it may be my cousin Oscar, or one of Oscar's children, or someone else entirely." He became quiet, brooding like he did sometimes.

It seemed like he was going to fret about a future that he couldn't effect. She leaned forward and said quietly in his ear, "You know, I haven't seen my husband in three days. Maybe I should send Blaga home for the night and we can... we can make our own dinner."

At this he sat up straight and turned to look at her. "I'm covered in sand flea bites. And this medicine smells horrible."

She smiled and winked. "There's nowhere left for me to make a mark?"

He stood up suddenly and reached for his shirt. "*Molim Vas, dodite, Blaga!*" Whatever that meant, within minutes, they were alone.

June 24, 1384 — If my reckoning is right, today marks the third year since we arrived, lost and without resources on Brijuni. As I look around our apartment here in Rovinj, I can't believe how short the eternity has been by the calendar, and how far home is by the same measure.

Marko took me to see the property this week. It is a shock to see how it has changed since... well, since I was last there. Once again, I find myself reticent to record too much about... about our time before that fateful date three years ago this day, lest someone find this diary and learn our secret. (Will you look at the formal tone of my writing here? Who is this woman I have become? No one here speaks English besides Marko and the occasional traveler, and those that come through are barely understandable. Yet I find myself writing things down in such a pompous manner, as if I'm recording some tome of literary worth! I resolve to be more... more the person I was before, at least here.)

As I was saying, the property. It's beautiful in its wild form, and it will be amazing to live there when the main house is complete. Marko has constructed a small log cabin that looks like something out of the ~~American~~ expansion phase of... well, I imagine a woodsman living there. It's cozy, though, and warm, and it keeps the creatures away. Mostly the fleas, ticks, midges, and whatever else plagues a person who sleeps on the ground without a tent. We will keep the apartment in Rovinj, even after the house is built, at least for a while. It's about three hours by walking or carriage, though a bit less by horseback, from here to there. It's hard to imagine, so much time for so little distance.

The strait that provided entry into the Venetian lagoon was a welcome sight to Celeste after a long day at sea. They left Rovinj at sun up, and caught what was predicted by the fishermen to be a strong wind blowing in the direction of the capital. By the time they arrived, the sun was low on the mountains of Italy, nearly ready to set.

Warships guarded the strait but didn't interfere with their little boat as it zipped along on the evening breeze, flying the flag of the Venetian empire. Gone was the fifty-kilometer-long sea wall that protected the lagoon from the open sea, with its massive floating locks that provided entry and exit from the below-sea-level waterways that gave Venice its unique quality. Of course, in the twenty-third century, several of the world's cities were partially submerged. But Venice had been since time immemorial, and that made it special.

They found moorage for the boat, and shortly thereafter lodgings, both near their destination. The next morning they found their way along the winding alleyways near the *Ponte de Rialto* to the offices of Francisco Alberti, a banker whose reputation as someone of extreme trustworthiness and capability extended as far as Rovinj and, given that they got the reference from the Novaks, even Dubrovnik.

"*Signora* Horvat, how may I help you?" asked the small man behind the expansive desk. Conservatively dressed, the man held himself with confidence, a trait that gave Celeste assurance that they had chosen correctly. Alberti glanced momentarily at Marko, who stood just inside the office door, then redirected his attention back to Celeste. He looked unsure whether or not to address Marko.

She held out a sealed letter, one of introduction from the Novaks, though there was no way she could directly hand it to him across the expanse of the desk. Instead she laid it on the desk and gave it a gentle push so it was within his reach. He picked up the letter, broke the seal, and read its contents quickly. He looked up and said, "There is not much here that gives clear detail to what you and..." He looked to Marko, as if undecided how to identify him.

Celeste, who expected to be sidelined once the conversation began, put an assertive tone in her voice and said, "My husband Marko and I are interested in establishing a significant account with your firm, with the intent that you should aid us in managing our investments so that we do not need to be directly involved with the day-to-day aspects of the businesses, yet have the ability to guide the investments when we, and our descendants, deem it necessary." Celeste turned so she included Marko in her audience, even though his Latin wasn't sufficient to follow the details of what she was saying. Marko's face was impassive.

Her statement brought Alberti's attention fully back to her. "You say a *significant* investment, *Signora* Horvat. How significant do you mean?" His tone and body language suggested he was talking down to a child who wasn't entirely clear what they were asking.

Celeste reached into her cloak, pulled out a heavy pouch, and dropped it on his desk where it made a loud, jangling thud. "*Signor* Alberti, please tell me what you can about these coins."

Alberti retrieved the pouch and opened it, pouring a few coins into his hand. With a small gasp, he said, "These are ancient, though I'm somewhat familiar with them. Depending on their purity, they are worth perhaps two to a *florin*."

"We live in Rovinj," Celeste said. "The common coin there is the *ducat*." Why couldn't these people settle on a single form of currency?

Alberti pursed his lips some, as if it frustrated him to be corrected. "The *ducat* and the *florin* are of similar value. Depending on the commission taken by the goldsmith to convert these to useable coin, as well as other factors that I can't address without further understanding of your situation, you can consider that you will receive between four and six modern coins for ten of these." He shook the pouch, weighing it in his hand. "There are perhaps one hundred of these coins in here? Even sixty *florins* is certainly no small amount of money, but it hardly makes for sufficient wealth to..."

"Please have someone evaluate those coins and let us know what conversion ratio we can expect."

"Certianly, *Signora*," Alberti said, with a somewhat patronizing tone. "However I..."

"We have ten thousand of these coins with which we wish to start our account."

"Ten *thousand, Signora*?" Now she had his attention. She waited just a moment before continuing, letting him wallow in the realization that he hadn't been appropriately respectful of her.

"I have not misspoken, *Signor* Alberti. Are you able to assist us?" She added just enough patronizing tone to her question to make it clear that she was displeased with him without creating tension that would end the meeting badly.

She turned to Marko and gestured. Marko moved his cloak to one side and unshouldered the custom box he commissioned that he carried on his back. The box was designed to lay close to his body so that it was near invisible under his cloak.

Wordlessly, Marko put the box on the desk with a decisive thud and released the catches, then opened it with a bit of a flourish. Inside were row upon row of gold coins identical to the ones in the pouch.

Alberti walked around the desk, apparently to get a better look. Marko, who towered over Alberti, moved to stand next to Celeste but kept the box, and Alberti, within arm's reach. Alberti looked at the coins, cleared his throat, then cleared it again. "I... I am certain that my firm can provide you with the assistance you require, *Signora*. Please tell me what sort of company you envision..."

They spent the rest of the day with Alberti and his functionaries, hammering out details of a quietly-run capital investment company that would take input from Marko and Celeste, and over time their descendants, but also have a certain level of autonomy in its activities. At several points, Alberti expressed surprise that people so young were as knowledgeable in the ways of business and finance as the Horvats.

They told him that they were raised in wealthy families and educated well their entire lives, which was true. The name Horvat was very common in Croatia, and so was 'Marko', so there was no way Alberti would be able to reliably investigate their claims. Neither of them brought up the name Foscari out of fear that Alberti might know someone in that family and start asking questions.

The company, once established, would invest in projects and businesses that furthered human advancement, with agriculture, shipping, and housing as the primary areas of focus. No investments would be made in companies with any business in war or warfare, weapons, or anything related. Investments would be conservative, though new ideas and discoveries would be encouraged and supported.

Finally, Celeste and Marko would have an allowance that allowed them to live comfortably, if not lavishly. And letters of credit would be sent to Rovinj that made funds available for construction of the estate house.

When pressed about the origin of the coins, Marko, through Celeste, would only say that they were a legacy of his family that had, for too long, sat idle. Alberti seemed to accept this explanation, and said no more about the subject.

Marko and Celeste returned to their lodgings exhausted, ate dinner, and retired early. As giddy as they were about the successes of the day, neither felt that they would be able to sleep. However, once they settled in, sleep took them both almost immediately.

They spent two more days in Venice waiting for valuation of their deposit with Alberti, though with nothing required of them, they spent the time taking in the sights of a city that defied sense in so many ways.

What surprised them most was how little Venice had changed over the nine century gap between times. The lagoon water, lower now than it was in the twenty-third century despite the efforts of the sea wall engineers, was dirtier in ancient Venice than it was in modern Venice. The introduction of sewage management systems and more responsible stewardship of the natural resource was certainly responsible. And of course, the neon signs, digital displays, and holographic projections were no longer here. But the basic set of the city was the same, and many buildings were familiar to the couple as they wandered the alleyways and bridges.

Fair winds and a good tide carried them back across the Adriatic Sea on the fifth day after they arrived in Venice. They carried with them letters of credit, a small cache of modern coins to use for expenses while investments were being established, and the security of knowing that there was enough wealth behind them that their future, and the future of nine hundred years of Horvat descendants, was secure.

Shortly after they left the lagoon and cleared the phalanx of warships that guarded it, Marko reached into a pocket and retrieved a small velvet bundle. One hand on the tiller, he extended his other and gave the small package, wrapped in a silk ribbon, to Celeste. She looked at him questioningly. He smiled back at her and said nothing.

Carefully she untied the ribbon and unwrapped a small box. She lifted the lid and there, glistening in the morning light, was the necklace she sold in Pula what felt like a lifetime ago. A wave of emotion rose from her belly and threatened to overcome her. Tears flowed freely down her face and immediately dried in the wind, only to be replaced by more. She looked up and saw him beaming back at her. "Where did you find this?" she finally choked out.

"I spotted it in one of the shops we stopped in. I didn't say anything at the time, as I wanted to surprise you. I went out last night after dinner and purchased it. It was... not inexpensive."

She didn't like it when he was evasive. "How much was it?"

"To my way of thinking, the price didn't matter. I'm still not clear on the value conversion between a *florin* and a *ducat*, but it was two hundred florins. Alberti, I'm certain, will think me foolish when he gets the bill."

"Two hundred florins? Marko!" She was shocked that he would spend what amounted to a lifelong fortune for many. It seemed irresponsible to her.

"You deserve to be made whole, my love. I would have spent twice that much and more."

She couldn't find any words to say, and instead sat there, tears streaming down her face and mixing with the salt spray as it came over the side of the boat. Knots formed in her chest as she contemplated Marko and the gift he had given her. As far as they were from home and family, she couldn't imagine being any happier in life.

"So, you are an architect?" Damir Stolar shuffled through the sheaf of drawings on his desk as Marko looked around the room. The walls were tastefully hung with drawings of example buildings. There was a faint odor of spice in the air mixed with smells of paper and ink.

"I have studied architecture some," said Marko. He was proud of his drawings, but reticent to call them excellent or even professional. The man before him was a master builder responsible for several stately homes and a handful of commercial buildings in the area. His offices in Poreč, where Marko sailed that morning, were clean, well appointed, and hopefully reflective of his work. Most importantly, the man had a reputation for a willingness to work with his clients to achieve their vision, or so it was reported by the people who provided Celeste with his name.

Celeste's ability to network with people and find the resources they needed amazed Marko. He thought of himself as reasonably sociable; he liked people just fine, but he didn't have the social insight she did that gave her the ability to ask *just the right question* to get the answer she needed and not seem like she was interrogating someone.

She once referred to Marko as "direct," which he took to mean "too blunt for polite society." He decided then that he would rely on her for things requiring intrigue, subterfuge, or anything beyond basic polite conversation. And she once again came to his rescue after he engaged a builder in Rovinj who, as it turned out, had a reputation for cost overruns, poor build quality, and unscrupulous business practices, even among those who considered their projects successes. After leaving it to her to find a reputable builder, Marko at least had confidence that he could carry on from there.

To Stolar he said, "The home we build should not only be sturdy enough to stand the test of time, but capable of adapting to the needs of future generations."

The man looked at Marko curiously. "What needs do you think these future generations might have of a home that doesn't include reliable shelter?"

Marko was disappointed with the man's question. Had he made the right choice in sailing almost three hours to see him? "Think of buildings that were built two or three centuries ago, and think about how different they are than buildings constructed today. Now look at the buildings constructed here, and compare them to what is being built in Venice, Florence, or Naples. The world is changing, and I expect it to keep changing. I want my children's children to have a home they can live in."

The man nodded, and returned to study Marko's drawings. "There are things shown here that I admit I do not understand, however they do not seem impossible. I have heard that in Ragusa, they now require closed coffers that capture the solid material in waste water before it enters the sea." So, Marko mused, Ragusa, or Dubrovnik really, was a leader in sewage treatment. All the better.

"The land I have purchased borders a swamp," Marko said. "Waste water should be sent there, as shown by that line that leads north and east on the site plan." Marko pointed to a place on one of the larger sheets of vellum.

A few weeks later, in late September, the green leaves of the forest turned to brilliant colors that ranged from golden russet to brilliant reds and yellows. Woodcutters fell trees and stacked logs that would be seasoned over winter and milled into lumber in the spring. Road builders worked to lay the track that would one day be the estate's grand drive. For now, it was a service road that would let an army of stonemasons, carpenters, and other tradesmen commute to and from Rovinj, Peroj, and even Pula.

Stonecutters made stacks of block, mined straight from the small hill that apparently existed where the villa would one day stand. Clay was mined to construct a kiln where waste wood was burnt with limestone offcuts from block making to create barrel after barrel of quicklime, which were then filled with water to create hydrated lime and, much to Marko's surprise, an immense amount of heat. It was one thing to know about exothermic reactions, and quite another to experience them. The stonemasons only knew that the heat, trapped in the rocks from the fire, came out when you added water. They laughed at his surprise and dared him to put his hand in the barrel.

Seven weeks were spent clearing the land and readying resources before weather forced the work to stop. Marko stood with Damir on the spot that would become the grand terrace overlooking the sea when a sudden rush of emotion overtook him. As much as he told himself that he was happy to make a life wherever Celeste was with him, standing here on the site where he grew up, where his mother watched him race from one tree to another to demonstrate how fast he could run, and where his father taught him to swim in the sea without choking on waves when they splashed against his face, brought to the surface a longing that he thought was buried forever. Damir looked at him and said, "It is going to be beautiful."

With a lump in his throat, Marko said, "You have no idea."

January 4, 1387 - I believe it's Thursday, though I can't be sure.

This winter has been cold and dark; the worst one since we arrived here. People seem to be in high spirits, though, as all of our little neighborhood and the rest of Rovinj are bustling with parties and other celebrations of the Christmas season. It's hard not to feel some of the joy these people do when they celebrate the birth of their icon.

Going to church, veritably a social requirement here, has been an odd experience. Venetians, and by extension the people of Rovinj, are staunchly Roman Catholic. My light experience with Christianity was that of a ~~Prot~~ ... well, it was different than this. I was quite unaware of the pomp and circumstance involved with a weekly trip to a place with the sole purpose that we be told how to act. Marko bears it stoically. A chapel will be built on the estate grounds, and maybe we can escape the cultish nature of the full Sunday service once we've moved there.

When I think of the constant state of war in much of the world, with the Venetians and the Habsburgs holding each other at arm's length, all the while fighting skirmishes with the insurgent Ottoman Empire, all of whom tell the world they're fighting for their version of God when they're really just trying to impose their will on the largest part of the world they can, it's hard not to consider that the relative peace in our little corner of it all is something of a miracle.*

Perhaps it's because of all these festivities and the high spirits that I'm so concerned about Marko. Work at the estate has halted for the winter, certainly at least during Christmas, but it really won't start up again for at least six weeks. Damir assures us that everything is going amazingly well, and attributes much of the success to Marko's input. He has been trying to get Marko to consult, for lack of a better word, on other projects. My husband is single-minded, however, and cannot see anything past the bounds of the estate property. In early December, he spent an entire week alone at the little cabin, and came back in worse shape than when he left.

Nothing seems to inspire him. I would think that the project of building a home that he knows will stand for ~~nearly a thousa~~ a very long time would inspire him, but he just seems to be moving through life without that spark in his eyes that I fell in love with those many years ago. He barely speaks to me, and our bed is cold most nights because he sits in his office staring into the dark. I'm not sure what to do.

We have invitations to three formal dinners celebrating Twelfth Night. I don't know how to choose. Whichever we attend, I hope Marko will at least appear to have a good time.

** Indeed the Venetians and the Habsburgs are both Christian, or say they are, while the Ottomans are Muslim.*

Damir and his crew seemed to have things well in hand. Construction started in late March, with most of the prep work out of the way the previous year, and work was proceeding quickly. It would still take all summer and into the fall to finish the shell of the house, though once it was complete the interior work could continue through the winter, which was much wetter and colder in the fourteenth century than it had been in the twenty-third.

Marko hated the cold, and wished that, in the dead of winter, they could climb aboard a jet plane and fly to Mauritius or Bora Bora, the latter of which would still have beaches, the sea having not yet risen. But Spring was upon them, and the chill of Winter was retreating. Marko felt a warmth in his soul that hadn't been there for months. Progress!

By midsummer, the walls were up and the roof trusses were being installed. Constructed from giant oaken beams imported from Poland, lifting them in place took three sturdy men climbing the hamster-wheel eternal ladder that formed the engine of a crane.

Marko watched as the fourth truss was lifted into place. The first three went up without incident, but a morning breeze sprung up, and it blew this one back and forth at the end of its tether. The crane, a rudimentary but effective device, couldn't respond quickly enough to the whipping wind, and the truss swung more wildly each moment.

"Bring it back!" shouted Damir. "Set it down!" The crane operator shouted instructions to his crew, and they responded quickly. The base of the crane began to turn, which in turn caused the truss to spin.

The momentum proved too much for the men holding the guide ropes, and soon the truss was swinging free. Marko watched in horror as the truss plowed into a high wall, pushing huge blocks out of their seats and shattering a stone lintel. A man screamed when a block fell on him, a high-pitched wail that told of pain unimaginable, and pushed him to the ground. The truss continued to swing, clattering against the sides of the wound in the wall, creating more damage as it did.

"Bring it down!" shouted Damir. "Drop it there!"

The crane operator grabbed a hammer and knocked the gear dog loose from its seat. The spool, free from restraint, unreeled as its load pulled several rounds of wrist-thick rope from its spindle. The truss dropped, and settled into the crevice it carved in the wall. Small stones, chips from the larger blocks, skittered down the wall to bounce off of their predecessors.

Damir and Marko, as well as several others, ran to the aid of the man pinned by the block. His screams of agony subsided some, but not completely. His left leg, from mid-thigh down, was trapped under most of what remained of the lintel. Damir gave orders, and three men with poles lifted the stone free as the poor man's screams resumed in earnest. What was revealed looked grim.

Marko fished in a coat pocket and removed a small, flat bottle, which he uncorked as he knelt next to the man.

"What's that?" asked Damir.

"Whiskey," replied Marko. "Like brandy, but from grain." He held the man's head and poured some in his mouth between moans of agony.

At first the man sputtered, then looked at Marko and said, "More." The crane operator provided a jacket, rolled into a pillow. The bottle was emptied and Marko laid the man's head onto the jacket, then stood.

Damir had a grim look on his face. "The potency of your elixir... what did you call it?"

"Whiskey."

"Whiskey, yes. It may make him feel better in the moment, but he will lose that leg."

"Does he have family?" Marko asked.

"A wife, yes, and two boys, I believe," said Damir.

"How will he provide for them?"

Both men jumped when the injured man, who was being loaded onto a hastily-constructed litter by his cremates, screamed again. "Get him to Rovinj," Damir said.

Two of the crew lifted the litter while two others went for a team of horses and a wagon. "Wait," said Marko, "set him back down." The litter bearers complied, and Marko used his knife to deftly cut the injured man's pant leg along its seam, then cut the boot from his foot. What he revealed barely looked human. The foot and ankle were twisted and misshapen, and everything below the knee was the color of eggplant. Marko prodded along the man's thigh and watched his face for a response. The whiskey hadn't taken effect yet, and the man looked at Marko curiously, but evidenced no pain. A prod below the knee produced a startled look and a wince. Below that, the shin was clearly beyond repair.

"Get me a length of cord as long as a forearm and that long peg over there," Marko snapped at one of the men. When he had what he asked for, he fashioned a tourniquet and twisted it tight on the man's shin, fixing it in place with a strip of cloth from the wrecked pants. "Tell the surgeon to cut below that first before taking any more of the leg."

The crew loaded their injured cremate into the wagon and watched solemnly as he was driven away. "You've seen this sort of thing before," said Damir.

"I have," Marko lied. "His foot was swelling up like a balloon, and it was clear it wouldn't be saved, but if his knee can be preserved, his life will be better."

"A... balloon?" Damir asked.

"Never mind that." He gestured to the devastation crowned by the rogue truss, trying to distract Damir from further inquiry. "What will we do about this?"

Damir frowned. "Things were going well," he said. "Too well, maybe. This will be a setback, you can be certain."

Marko looked wistfully at the empty bottle in his hand. He tipped it up and watched a few drops fall to the ground. "I should return to Rovinj. I think more of this will be necessary."

Marko sat on the balcony of their apartment and stared down the length of the street at the tiny sliver of ocean that could be seen. The view calmed him, and he stared at it for hours as the mug of tea somehow grew colder than the air around it.

His head hurt from last night's drinking; sleep was increasingly expensive in both whiskey and hangovers, but compared to lying awake, thoughts churning like a turbid eddy, it was well worth the price. Something in Marko realized that he was on the verge of having a problem there, but it was just one more problem in the stack, and didn't stick out any more than the rest.

Celeste came up from behind, put her arms around him, and kissed him gently on the neck, warming his mood. "Blaga will have lunch ready soon, my dear. Will you dress and eat in the dining room?"

Marko turned to look at her. Lunch? Had he eaten breakfast? He couldn't remember. He looked down at himself, at the dressing robe, briefs, and lightweight sandals, then back to Celeste. Her green eyes looked back at him, gentle and imploring. No one but Marko would have seen the worry behind those eyes, her silent plea for him to drag himself out of the pit of despair he'd dug. He hadn't told her of his troubles, but he could tell she knew. That sort of knowing was part of her.

He turned to look at himself again, sniffed, and said, "I suppose if I'm going to appear civilized, I should bathe. Is there time?"

She smiled, and it warmed him more than the mid-day sun could. She reached out and put a hand on his face. "There is. Maybe even enough time to shave. I'll have Blaga put on a kettle to warm a bath."

He gently pushed her hand aside with his own, and felt the stubble... beard? When did he grow a beard? Maybe the apartment needed more mirrors. But then, maybe it didn't. They tended to show people at their worst.

He shaved at the dressing table, then cleaned the basin and replaced it. Everything he did felt methodical. The outlook of the day held nothing for him. He wrapped the robe tightly around him so he wouldn't scandalize Blaga (though he was hard pressed to think of something that would), and went downstairs.

With each step, the weight of his mood settled around him, dark and foreboding. It became something akin to comfortable. The bathroom, literally the room for the bath, was behind the kitchen, a renovation Marko put in when they bought the apartment. It included a floor drain where all the household waste could be sent on its way, into a sewer tunnel that emptied into the sea. A wax plug kept the stench and the rats at bay, and Blaga seemed happy with the whole arrangement.

The hot water felt good against his skin as he lowered into the tub. He dipped a handful of the gooey concoction that passed for soap from the crockery on the shelf and began to wash mechanically, allowing his hands to follow well-practiced paths. His mind wandered, and soon the water was cold. He could hear Blaga and Celeste on the other side of the wall talking in low tones. He had no idea how long he'd been there.

With a sigh he pulled the plug and watched the water run out, listened to it as it cascaded over the edge of the floor drain and... oh, no, the floor drain. Wincing, he lifted himself out of the bronze tub and squatted next to the now-overflowing drain, thinking that he should have replaced the plug in the tub; the water was threatening to run into the kitchen. He plunged his hand into the drain and found the stopper, then pulled it free. A bubble of sewer gas assaulted his nose as the water rushed down the hole, and he wished for the thousandth or millionth time for modern plumbing and sanitation.

He dried himself with a towel and found that Celeste, or likely Blaga, left him some clean clothes. He dressed numbly, and opened the door to find Celeste and Blaga staring at him. Celeste's face was placid, but Blaga's had worry writ large. "Did I miss lunch?" he asked.

"You're worried," Marko said.

Celeste maintained her look of calm, but her eyes were wet. The corners of her mouth turned down slightly as she nodded. They were seated at the dining table, and not the kitchen table where they normally took their lunch. This insulated them some from Blaga, who was in the kitchen, occasionally peering through the doorway, checking more often than was necessary for a sign that she was needed. And they were speaking English rather than Croatian, which added another layer of insulation.

Marko looked down at his plate. Lunch should be delicious, and it was clear that Blaga had put in extra effort today. But the few bites he'd taken tasted like ash in his mouth. Chewing and swallowing were things he did by memory rather than anything else.

"I know you're... upset by the setbacks at the estate," said Celeste. "But I've read Damir's reports, and things are going well. The walls are up, the roof is on, and the glass windows from Murano have been fitted..." She trailed off. "Marko, look at me."

He looked at her rather than... well, he heard it called a 'thousand meter stare,' and supposed it applied to one of a thousand years as well. Looking at Celeste brought him back to the present, which was the last place he wanted to be were it not for her.

"Look at me, Marko," she repeated. She reached out and took his hand in hers. Her hands were warm, contrasting the numbing cold of his own. "I don't know what has you in its grips, and I don't know what I can do to help you. If you tell me, maybe I can help. Is it the estate?"

He formed an unsure smile, though it was one of irony rather than mirth. "It is and it isn't," he said, and reached for the glass of wine Blaga poured him earlier. The wine was strong, and he could feel his nerves steadying as it rushed down his throat. He paused for a moment, trying to order his thoughts so he could make her understand. She waited for him.

"When that man, Josip, was injured, he could have died."

"But he didn't," she said. "Your quick action probably saved his life, and certainly saved his leg enough that..."

"He didn't have to," he said.

She stopped what she was saying, looked oddly at him, then asked, "Didn't have to... what? Get injured? It was an accident."

"A preventable one. A better, more modern crane..."

"Shh... Marko, please, Blaga understands more English than she lets on. Maybe not enough to understand what you're saying, but she's no dullard either."

He looked through the kitchen door to find Blaga seated at the small table there, apparently having lunch of her own, smiling at him. He smiled back, and she pretended interest in her meal. Marko sighed and lowered his voice, then leaned toward Celeste. She smelled like flowers.

"A better crane would have prevented his injury, given him the ability to provide for his family and live a good life."

"You can't know that. Workplace injuries happen in our own ti... back home as well. These people understand what they're getting into when they take the job."

These people? That didn't sound like the woman he had traveled back in time with, so concerned over how a young girl at a hotel perceived herself to be lesser than the apparent upper class people she was serving. Celeste, it seemed, changed in their six years of temporal imprisonment. Had he changed, and if so in what ways?

He looked at her as he took another drink of wine. He paused to stare at the glass for a moment, and considered that in his hand might be one of the ways he'd changed. He dismissed the thought as not part of their current conversation, a distraction. He looked back at her. He couldn't see anything in her eyes to indicate she recognized what she'd said. "You may be right," he said. "But what of the man? Of his family? We owe him a debt."

She nodded in response, as if grudgingly agreeing with him. "I will write to Damir and ask him what became of... Josip? Is that his name?"

Marko nodded in response. How could she not remember the name of the man who sacrificed a part of himself in their service?

They stared at each other for several seconds, not eating, not saying anything. Part of Marko wanted to take her to task for her lack of compassion, and another part of him thought it wouldn't matter. These two parts warred for attention in his head with the ones that wanted to scream out everything that was wrong in his life. But the part that knew none of it would change held the line and kept him silent.

Finally he took a deep breath, let it out slowly, and said, "It's not just Josip. I'm concerned for him, certainly, but it's... everything. Since we arrived here, or at least since we found the treasure, I've been focused on building the house. I had purpose, and the obstacles, like not having indoor plumbing, decent transportation, or access to information, all seemed like problems that could be overcome..."

"You did overcome them, my love. Look what is being built! Who but you could have achieved that?"

He sighed. She was missing his point. "Yes, I overcame them. And the estate house is being built, just the way I remember it. Damir and his crew are doing an amazing job following my plans, even if they don't understand some of my reasons for doing things, and mine are the drawings of a complete amateur. My brain turns in knots when I think about how this all came about. But the obstacles remain, and once the house is finished, then what?"

She looked at him for a moment before responding. "I've thought about this a lot. I think we should buy a ship and travel the world."

The war in his brain collapsed, a ceasefire declared. He began to think about a ship, a yacht, really, designed to let them travel in comfort from place to place, never anywhere long enough for anyone to question their apparent lack of aging. The could see the world, helping people where they could. They would need crew, but crew on a ship came and went. He imagined them going from port to port, through India, China, and Japan, staying as long as they cared but not too long. In a few decades, after they had been long forgotten by the people who knew them now, they could return to the estate and work out how to ensure it stayed in the family for centuries to come.

They made love that afternoon, with a vigor not present in years. The sun streamed in the open terrace doors, warmed their naked bodies, and made the room glow. At one point, Marko applied himself with an energy he never had before. Celeste cried out in pleasure, then laughed and told him, between barely-suppressed moans, that if they weren't careful, the entire island would hear them. "I don't care!" proclaimed Marko. "Let the world hear us, let them know we are alive!"

BLAGA sat at the small table in the kitchen and watched her charges through the kitchen door, idly chewing on a piece of fresh bread. Master Marko was so depressed lately. She was worried for him, as was Lady Celeste. If only they were her children, she thought, she would know what to do. But they weren't, and she had to be careful not to take a rough tone with them the way she would with her own family, particularly that layabout husband of hers.

She watched and listened. Their conversations were always in English when they didn't want to be understood; to keep their secrets. Blaga understood a few words of their language, but not enough to follow the conversation.

What she did understand was, while Lady Celeste claimed to be from Trieste, and Master Marko from somewhere south, near Split, the language they spoke was from nowhere near here, and they spoke it like natives. And when he spoke the Croat language, it was with an accent she had never heard before, even from her cousin, who grew up in Šibenik, or the Novaks, who were from Dalmatia.

As Blaga listened, Master Marko looked at her and smiled. It was good to see him smile, but it was clear that he was checking to see if she was listening, the way she had done with her children when they were young. She smiled back, hoping to say, "Oh, don't mind me, I'm just here eating my lunch" with her look. Master and Lady lowered their voices and leaned closer to one another, and Blaga decided that if she were out of sight, they might relax some and she would be able to hear them once again.

Blaga held no disrespect for her charges. In fact, she loved them as if they were her own. They were so kind to her these many years, not like her previous employer who had been so horrible. It was clear that Master and Lady, as young as they were, had secrets they didn't want any to know, and Blaga would keep those secrets if she knew them. But she loved a mystery, and loved to fill in blanks where information wasn't available. Who was hurt, if she never told anyone?

She thought about what she knew. Beyond the language issue, which made it seem like they grew up somewhere far away, she could see that he was born of parents from this part of the world. Her olive skin and dark hair made her look Genoese, though more beautiful than any she had seen before.

Blaga wished her eldest son had found someone as beautiful as Lady Celeste rather than that hag he married in a hurry before the baby started to show. But people that beautiful were destined for husbands that were not her son; handsome like Master Marko, and rich like him too.

They tried to hide their wealth, perhaps because there would be questions, but Blaga could see that no question of money crossed their mind when they chose furniture, made modifications to the house (oh, how she loved Master Marko's innovations), or paid their employees. Blaga wished that bitch Sanja appreciated Master and Lady more than she did. Sanja flitted in and out of the house, doing only what was required of her two days a week, barely saying a word to anyone. The least she could do was show some gratitude. Blaga resolved to take her to task the next time Sanja came to clean.

Nothing could be heard any longer from the next room, and when Blaga looked, no one was there. Master and Lady must have retired to their rooms upstairs. Blaga cleaned up the remains of lunch, so carefully prepared and only partially eaten, and continued her musing.

Once, many years ago, she overheard a conversation, again in this English language they used, where they mentioned *"gradina"*. Blaga wondered at the time if it was the same *gradina* her mother told her about, on the island of Brijuni, near Pula.

Her mother said that it was a place where the old gods hid from the new world and Christendom, waiting for the day when they were called forth again. People, it was said, would go up there and make offerings; people who said they had Christ in their hearts, but wanted an extra measure of support for their prayers. Could Master and Lady be some of those old gods, come forth into the world?

Blaga knew they had the same issues as any human. Master Marko bled when he cut himself shaving, but then didn't Christ bleed when his tormenters put the crown of thorns on his head? What did she know of the way of gods? She knew Master and Lady were kind, though, and so long as Blaga held Christ in her heart, she would take care of Marko and Celeste in the best way she could. Maybe, if she was lucky, they would grant her favor without her asking. Only time would tell.

Tuesday, August 14th, 1388 - Moving day.

The estate house is complete, and we are moving in today. Blaga has prepared a wonderful breakfast, and the drayage men will arrive late this morning. The furniture was delivered last week, and the house was made ready for us yesterday. Marko is beside himself. I'm excited, too, though life without Blaga, who has become like family these past five years, will be a hard adjustment. The distance from her home to our new one is just too far, and her husband is determined to stay where he is.

In a month or so I would like to host a party to open the house. Damir would come, as it would be good for his business to show off what he has created. And Alberti would come over from Venice to see where our money has been spent. My heart would like to invite Lagorio and Agata, but how would we explain ourselves? What if there were trouble? I think I'll surprise Marko and invite Grga and the rest from Trieste. Won't he be shocked?!?

Josip leaned on his crutches and shouted orders at his two sons. He kept adjusting the left crutch, which was causing discomfort in his armpit. Three years after he'd lost the leg, he could get around pretty well with the fancy replacement Master Marko commissioned for him, so long as he was indoors or on even ground. Here on the roadway, a stone the size of an avocado pit could send him crashing, and the last thing he was going to let happen was to have his boys or that piss-poor friend of theirs who worked with them — if you could call it work — see him at a disadvantage.

"Tap gently on that stone, you idjit! You want to hammer out a replacement because you were too impatient to set it right? Remind me when we get home, I'll talk to your ma about hammering out a replacement for you!" He loved his boys, but God's grace, they were imbeciles sometimes. Where they got it he would never know. Probably from their mother's side. That brother of hers was daft as a drunken squirrel, and about as useful.

He heard a muffled laugh, and turned to see the carpenter crew, sitting on their pile of lumber having their lunch, clearly entertained by the sight of he and his boys. Ire rose in him, and he turned it toward the lumbermen. "You think it's funny, that? I see you sitting there, idling away the afternoon while my boys sweat in the sun. You don't have to wait for them to finish to get started, and that scaffolding isn't going to build itself. Master Marko pays you for a day's work, and imma see you give it to him one way or the other!" He dropped his right crutch, reached for the hammer at his belt, and suddenly lunches disappeared into pockets and break was over.

With that settled, he surveyed the drawings laid out on his worktable. They were beautiful, with little insets to show the details that might be missed in the larger drawings. Damir's scribes, aided by Master Marko, worked long hours to produce exacting detail that showed how to build the main gatehouse, and Josip wasn't going to have it screwed up by sloth and slovenliness, no way.

His gaze lingered as he considered the massive keystone at the top of the gateway arch, and the riggers that would lift it into place. Josip was going to be sure he was far enough from the situation to keep out of any accidents that happened, but close enough to make sure the work got done right. And if even the slightest breeze came up, well, he'd show them how a one-legged man could run.

"Happy anniversary, my love," said Celeste.

"Happy anniversary to you," Marko replied. They took their evening meal on the veranda. The cook prepared lamb chops, laid artfully across a pile of new potatoes and dried plums and a tiny bowl of *ajvar*, a favorite of Marko's, on the side. A salad of mixed greens, grown in the garden, and soft goat cheese from the neighbor's smallholding, completed their meal. Later there would be dessert, served just in time to watch the sun sink into the sea from the little gazebo on the point.

The point had not existed, at least not above sea level, when Marko was a boy. Back then, from where they sat on the veranda, the sea wall was less than a dozen meters away. Today, nine hundred-odd years in the past, ten years to the day since Marko had last seen his home, the waves lapped gently against the shore fifty or more meters from the house.

"You'll be surprised to hear this," said Celeste, "but I received a letter from Petra yesterday. She evidently heard news of a Marko and Celeste Horvat, of Rovinj, having built a large house. She presumed it was us, and sent a letter of congratulations."

Marko smiled. When they last saw Petra, the first person they met after becoming trapped in the past, they posed as a debutante and her servant. That they were not who they said was probably no shock to Petra. "Did she say anything about how she's been the last decade?"

"She did. Her father evidently tried to marry her off to a baker a few years after we were there. Petra told him 'no' and there was evidently a couple years of grumbling over it. Ultimately she married a man of good standing, whom she says loves her, and she loves him. They have two small boys, which keep her busy, and have purchased a house, partly with funds she kept for herself over the years."

"That's a lot for one letter."

"It's been many years since we've seen her. I suppose a lot has happened. I wrote her back, telling her that indeed we are the people she remembers, and said we would arrange a time for them to come visit."

Marko told her that he would enjoy visiting with Petra's family. Since building the house, small children had been about occasionally. He and Celeste made it clear to their friends that youngsters were welcome in their home, even if they had none of their own. They both found joy in the excited squeals of little ones at play, though Marko cringed every time he heard a baby cry. The wails of a discontented child, for reasons he couldn't put his finger on, bothered him deeply.

He was resigned to the fact that he and Celeste would never have children, though they discussed adopting. But how would they explain their long lives to a child? Waiting until they were in the sunset of their lives, which might be three hundred or more years, seemed like an intolerable amount of time to do without children. And probably they would have soured on the idea by then anyway. Always they agreed to take up the conversation again when the time seemed better, though better times never seemed to come. Perhaps now that the house was complete they could discuss it again, though recently Marko had other ideas on his mind.

As the sun settled slowly into the sea, wispy clouds of pink, red, and blue spread the light across the water in a spectacular painting of an early summer evening. The light turned Celeste's dress a deep shade of purple that leaned slowly toward blue as the evening faded into night. Dessert, a delicious baked custard of goat's milk, honey, and eggs — so reported by the cook, who made a special trip out to the gazebo to deliver the delicacy rather than send one of his underlings — was rich and perfect for the occasion. Cicadas serenaded them as they ate, and when they were finished, Marko said, "You suggested last year that we build a ship and sail the world."

"I did. I know you've been designing one — a yacht, really."

He thought about the doodles he'd put to paper, festooned with notes about length and hull shape, sail plan and rigging; as many questions as answers. Shipwrights would be able to fill in the blanks, much like Damir had for the house. "Yes, I'm working on it. But I've been thinking about leaving... I mean, about how to set ourselves up to leave. That will take some planning."

She smiled the smile she did when someone else might sigh with exasperation, often reserved for times he suggested they make meticulous plans around something she was sure they could just jump into. Occasionally he relented and followed her lead, but this was important enough that he would stand his ground. Their eyes met, and a wordless exchange said everything that was needed about which path they would take. Finally she asked, "What do you propose?"

Every fireplace in the house burned bright; their heat kept the cold from an early winter snow at bay. The house bustled with activity as people found excuses to work indoors rather than out, and Celeste did her best to contribute despite the protestations of the entire staff. "This is your special day, Lady Celeste. You shouldn't have to lift a finger!"

"A party is for the people attending it; the guest of honor is merely an excuse," said Celeste, for what seemed like the hundredth time. Yes, it was her birthday, and she appreciated that everyone in the house wanted her to relax, but she felt more useful, more alive when she had something to do.

She was turning thirty. Growing up, thirty hadn't seemed like much of a milestone. She expected by then to be establishing her career, perhaps writing a book as a side project and working for a charitable organization or maybe for the government.

The UDNG employed a large outreach arm, always encouraging independent states to join their ranks, with particular focus on what remained of Real America. In no way could she have imagined the life she was given, trapped as they were in a Renaissance world with no access to even the simplest technologies, surrounded by people who didn't understand the world outside their own city, or for that matter just how big the world was.

If she remembered correctly, North and South America wouldn't be discovered for another hundred years, and Australia sometime after that, at least by Europeans. And the native populations of any of those continents had little idea that Europe existed, though Celeste admitted that it was probably best for them they didn't, at least for now.

She brushed aside her wool gathering and focused on the party. She had sent invitations to about thirty people, about half of whom might show up, given the weather. But those that did brave the cold would bring companions, so they prepared for forty guests and hoped that would be enough.

When she and Marko first opened the house after construction was complete, Celeste established a tradition that the staff, who would be busy working to serve a house full of guests during a party, would have an early dinner, served from the same menu as the arriving guests. She recognized her station as head of the house, even if the fourteenth-century legal structure said that she would defer to Marko in all things. The staff recognized it too, and so did Marko, who was happy to be left designing his yacht. But she refused to treat the staff as anything but well-regarded employees who deserved everything they got and more, an attitude that confounded her contemporaries to the point that Celeste stopped discussing it with them.

In the three years since their move from Rovinj, Celeste worked to refine a set of operating principles for the house. A review by Marko found many large gaps, and she worked to fill those in. Smaller gaps were found by the youngest of Josip's three boys, age twelve. A precocious child, who both parents were certain took after the other, would grow up to be a either a defense lawyer or a con man given his ability to find even the smallest advantage in a situation.

Earlier in the year, she and Marko talked over plans for leaving the house for several decades, and realized the estate would need to be able to operate independently of them and their guiding hands. They refined the operating principles into a fully fledged manual that laid out roles and responsibilities, with Celeste getting guidance from the Novaks, who once spent two years on a trip to the Greek Isles, a trip nearly impossible now with the naval pressures from the Ottomans. Of course, Celeste hadn't mentioned how long she and Marko planned to be gone, but that they wanted the house to operate well without them, possibly for years at a time.

With the operation of the house in hand, they turned their attention to management of their little investment company. Regular letters from Alberti told them of the various investments that were made, which ones bore fruit, and which ones did not. On balance, the company made more money than it lost, and provided the Horvat household with more income than they needed. In the last year, the estate and its agricultural endeavors produced more than it consumed, selling the balance at local markets. This meant that their local bank account steadily grew, enough that the estate could weather most storms without drawing on company reserves.

Marko wrote Alberti over the summer and told him of their plans to build a yacht and sail the world. Alberti, of course, fretted that they just built the house, and wouldn't they just rather settle in and build a family instead, rather than running off on some grand adventure, risky as those were?

Several letters were exchanged, and within a few months Marko possessed bank notes that would pass in several port cities around the Mediterranean, England, and Germany. Celeste observed, with resigned amusement, that Alberti's idea of "the world" was unfortunately small. What about China, India, and the entirety of Africa? Trade had been going on there since the Romans.

She supposed that if she and Marko were really going to spend decades at sea, they would have sufficient time to figure out how to draw money from home. And while having coins and jewels with them was risky and inconvenient, no one would object to their value.

The party was a rousing success, even if attendance was lighter than expected. Someone brought two wheels of cheese, imported from France, and Celeste nearly fainted with delight. She hadn't tasted a blue cheese since she left home, and had forgotten how much she missed the sour tang on her tongue. Later, after the guests departed, she encouraged the staff to try some, and none would dare. The cook, a pious man, declared the proposition "against God," and refused to allow "the abomination" in the kitchen. Rather than press the issue, Celeste put the one remaining wheel in the cellar where it would keep at least until Spring.

Later, in their bedroom, they sat next to each other on a small sofa in front of a crackling fire. Something about the smell of the burning wood, the warmth of the fire on her face, and the flavor of the sweet wine they were drinking combined to make her feel romantic. Far away in the kitchen, the sounds of laughter and banging pots told her the house was alive. She snuggled against Marko, stretched as far as the sofa would let her, and hummed softly to herself.

After a few minutes, Marko leaned over and kissed her on the head. "I have an idea," he said.

She smiled, and reached up to rub his thigh. "I imagine you do."

His hand reached out and held hers, and he laughed softly. "Well, that's an idea for now. But I have another idea, one for the near future."

At this she sat up, nearly spilling her glass of wine. "An idea besides the yacht?" She searched his face for an answer.

"Yes." He paused, opened his mouth twice, paused again, then seemed to collect himself. "We've been here ten years. The house is complete, a company to ensure its long term viability is in place... in short, we've fulfilled the role we thought we needed to fulfill. I think we should return to the cave and try to go home."

Emotion welled up in her and threatened to make her cry. She pushed it down enough that only a single tear escaped to run down her cheek. "Home?" The concept was somewhat fleeting to her. She had spent a third of her life, her entire adulthood, here in the fourteenth century. Her childhood, however clearly she remembered it, seemed distant. Going back would be wonderful, though trying and failing would be hard to take. "What if it doesn't work?"

"Then we fall back to our current plan and sail the world." His tone wasn't exactly flippant, but the ease with which he could say such a thing somehow bothered her. How would he *feel* if it didn't work? She supposed, however, that he didn't think about how he'd feel until he felt it. From what she could tell, men were that way. Or at least hers was, and it appeared to be a common trait.

They talked long into the night about preparations, timing, and how the situation they left behind would survive without them. Finally, exhausted and with sore, dry throats, they retired, notions of romance long behind them. Marko blew out the bedside lamp and rolled over to face her. In the darkness, he said, "Happy birthday, my love. I hope my idea turns out to be a great gift and not a horrible joke." She kissed him gently, and hoped he didn't detect the tears that flowed freely, soaking her pillow with her fear of what might be.

October 8, 1391 — Marko's Gift

First I will tell you that the party to celebrate my thirtieth birthday was a success, even given the weather. Marko was evasive whenever he was asked about the carving on the beam, saying that the story was somewhat abbreviated due to space constraints, and in fact the treasure was found by his great grandparents and held in secret for generations until it was bequeathed to he and I as a wedding gift. He got better at the story with practice, but subterfuge is not his strong suit.

My real news is both exciting and frightening: Marko wants to return to the cave, and hopefully home from there. We have built the estate and established the company, and hopefully fulfilled our duties to the gods of the time stream. He says that if we fail, we will build a yacht and sail the world. I am trying to steel myself against the idea of failure, and I believe I have built up a certain tolerance to it in the many times we've tried to go home. We will make our attempt soon, so I won't have to worry for long.

The sun was high and the sky clear as they set out on the same journey they had in 2285. Rather than an automatically-guided power boat, they sailed the *Properus*, the sleek little runabout that served them so well for the last decade.

Cold waves splashed over the gunwale, driving Celeste to cower in the cargo box rather than endure the assault of the sea. Part of her felt bad for peering out from a position of relative comfort while Marko sailed, but his ability with the boat far outclassed hers, and he didn't appear to mind the cold. She supposed that his year as a drayage sailor in Trieste inured him to such indignities.

By mid-afternoon, they pulled into the little Brijuni bay and the wind subsided to a gentle breeze. With a sharp turn of the tiller and swing of the sail, Marko put the boat on the windward side of the pier next to the olive mill without having to resort to a paddle. Celeste marveled at the way he demonstrated casual skill at such things, as if he were born to sail and the boat was an extension of him.

They secured the boat against the weather, pulled their cloaks around them to ward off the cold, shouldered backpacks that contained a few supplies, as well as the volumes of Celeste's diaries, and followed the trail to the cave. Before they entered the forest, Celeste looked across the bay to the dilapidated ruin of the villa. So much had happened there in the last ten years. How would it have been different if, when Marko suggested they check out the hilltop ruins, she had suggested they take the boat to Pula? Where would they be now?

As Celeste trudged up the hill behind Marko, her feet sore from the cold and the weight on her back, she lamented having written so much over the years. Perhaps documenting their lives in such detail wasn't the best idea.

She also regretted not staying in better shape. At thirty years old, she should be able to make this hike with ease, even with a load on her back. Of course, she shouldn't have to do it weighed down by a heavy cloak and should have better quality shoes, but the fact remained that she had gone soft, something she resolved to change no matter the outcome of their adventure today.

Little changed at the *gradina* on the hilltop since their arrival. Two ribbons flitted in the breeze, both newer than the one they'd seen before, so someone had been there. At the cave, nothing looked different from any of the times they'd visited.

In the dirt outside the cave entrance, Celeste scribed a distinctive mark with the toe of her boot.

"What's that," Marko asked. "It looks like a rune of some sort. Did you learn witchcraft when I wasn't looking?"

"Not at all, unless you consider this marker, which will easily be washed away in the next rain, as a tell for whether or not we travel in time, to be witchcraft."

He nodded. "Makes sense. Good idea."

Marko took a small square lantern out of his pack and lit it. Celeste recognized it as a signaling lantern from a ship. Three sides were made from tinted glass, and a lens was set in the fourth side, which was clear. The lens formed a beam that could be directed ahead of them, much like a flashlight.

In the first chamber of the cave, Marko searched the walls. He said he was looking for signs that he might have missed before, as he had dozens of times before on their previous visits. Just like the other times, there was far less graffiti than they first encountered the cave in 2285, though some existed that looked Roman to her, and some other that looked newer than that.

They continued to the deepest part of the cave, where they surveyed the walls and examined the floor. It was clear that no one was here since they were nine years ago. The only footprints were their own.

Marko handed Celeste the lantern. "When we were first here, you were taking pictures with your slate, turning as you did. Do you remember which of the drawings you photographed?"

She couldn't remember much beyond taking a few random pictures and feeling sick to her stomach. Too much time had passed. "I don't. Do you think it's significant? And what of this?" she gestured with the lantern.

"I've been thinking that maybe shining light on certain drawings has something to do with the time travel mechanism, if there is one."

She wished momentarily that he'd thought of this years ago. But better now than never. She studied the drawings in earnest, shining the lantern on each, slowly turning in a circle. As she completed her turn, she shone the light in Marko's face and said, "I'm sorry, I don't..."

Before she could complete her sentence, she was overcome with a wave of nausea. She fought the urge to retch, and watched as Marko did the same. A wave of dizziness came over her, and she nearly dropped the lantern. She held onto it, though, and kept her feet under her. Marko staggered slightly, then turned to look at her with what she presumed was the same hope that she felt.

Without a word, Marko took the lantern from her, grabbed her hand, and headed for the mouth of the cave. It was dark outside, though that could mean they jumped forward no more than two hours rather than centuries. Or, Celeste shuddered to think, they could have jumped back again, a fear she did not address with Marko.

"Do you see the mark I made?" she asked.

He held the lantern high so the light shone on the trees around them. All were black, and the air smelled like a dead campfire. "I don't think the mark will be there," he said. All along the path back toward the *gradina*, the trees were nothing more than charred husks.

They picked their way along the trail, over the top of the hill and back down to the pier. In the light of the lamp, they couldn't see that the pier was different, except that *Properus* was gone. The air, which had borne the frigidity of winter no more than an hour ago, was cool and, now that they were out of the burned forest, smelled like Spring.

Marko turned in a circle, shining the lantern into the night.

"What now, your Lordship?" Celeste asked, and wished for him to hear the edge of teasing she put in to cover the concern she felt.

"What now, indeed," he said.

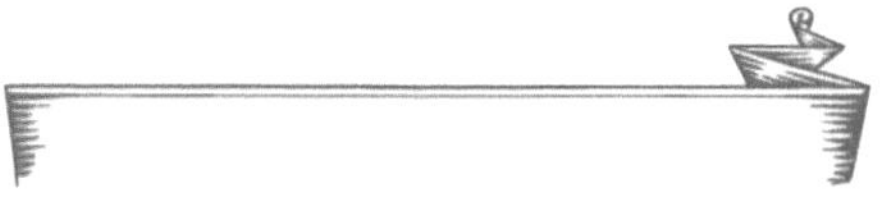

Thank You

Where have Marko and Celeste landed? Did they make it home? The adventure continues in Part Two.

Thank you for reading this story. It's the result of a long journey of learning to write. If you enjoyed it, I'm really happy that you did. Part Two is well underway. You can get news and updates by following Lives in Time on Facebook (facebook.com/livesintime[1]).

Thanks also goes to Steve Perry and Daniel Keys Moran, well-respected authors and (importantly) my true friends who took time to coach me through some rough patches. And, as mentioned in the dedication at the front of this work, the continuing efforts of the community at The Writing Forums[2], without whom I couldn't have made it this far.

But this novel would not have been at all possible without my wife Jennifer, who put spark to tinder by suggesting the idea for the story. Her patience with me as I spent long hours holed up in the world I had created, researching the history of various aspects of the story (the history of glass windows is a rabbit hole you probably don't want to go down) or fixing mechanical problems with the inner workings of the story, is what enabled me to get this far. I love her beyond measure, and look forward to our future adventures together.

---

1.   http://facebook.com/livesintime

2.   https://www.writingforums.org/

www.ingramcontent.com/pod-product-compliance
Lightning Source LLC
Chambersburg PA
CBHW051422130726
47989CB00014B/459